CW00687743

EXTORTION

The Whirlwind

LISETTE SKEET

Strategic Book Publishing and Rights Co.

Strategic Book Publishing and Rights Co., LLC
USA | Singapore
www.sbpra.net

For information about special discounts for bulk purchases, please contact Strategic Book Publishing and Rights Co., LLC Special Sales, at bookorder@sbpra.net.

ISBN: 978-1-68235-394-3

In Loving Memory of a Gentle Man

CONTENTS

INTRODUCTION

"Mary! I signed off! I don't even have benefits!"

"Re-register then," her sister persisted. "Or sign in again, or whatever it is you claimants have to do. Anyway, you haven't got a husband or a partner now, and you are on a low income. So, you can get benefits!"

Sarah felt as if it was getting hard to breathe.

As a result of traumatic experiences, all kinds of emotions influence the way in which an individual responds to new challenges. Such sensitivities develop and become habitual, and they may be referred to as *affects* in Freudian terms.

When habits are established during childhood, they become embedded in the unconscious mind of each person within the family. Those old ways may be repeated. Memories, both hidden and conscious, are carried all the way through the years and they can resurface at the worst possible times.

Sarah struggles to believe her sisters truly intend to treat her unkindly, and their extraordinary interest in her private financial affairs is a real shock. In fact, she hasn't forgotten the many times when feelings of confusion and unhappiness affected her younger self as a result of their actions, and it feels inevitable when those feelings return.

As a new situation unfolds, it seems the twins' potential for harmful behaviour never went away.

THE TALK

On a bright morning in April, Sarah travelled from her home town in Suffolk to a hospice on the outskirts of London. There, her brother was being nursed. She couldn't relax during her train journey, feeling anxious and wondering if he would seem very much changed. A telephone call had been worrying when his voice sounded hoarse and oddly unfamiliar.

Upon entering the ward, Sarah felt relieved. Jeff was there; she saw him at once. He was peacefully watching television. He looked wan, but his long, fair hair was neatly combed and he was clean-shaven. When his sister approached, he made efforts to sit up, punched pillows to lean on and turned with a lively expression to receive her kiss.

"Hello, Sis!"

She placed a parcel of fruit on his table before perching herself on a plastic chair, feeling both awkwardly out of place and relieved to be beside her brother again. Nervousness made her tremble. When she pulled a bottle of water from her bag, she lifted it to her lips and spilt some. Jeff handed her a bunch of tissues and she hastily pressed one on her damp skirt. She looked up and he smiled.

"You've still got beautiful eyes!"

A passing nurse overhead the remark and she glanced at Sarah with a friendly smile.

1

Sarah felt self-conscious. "Thanks!" She kept her eyes on her brother's face. He did sound hoarse when he spoke, but he seemed eager to chat, nonetheless.

Jeff explained that he hoped to leave the hospice soon. With plans to write about his travels, he had bought a new laptop. He was full of ideas for a collection of true stories and a book was already drafted!

"Really? You've been writing?" Sarah gently teased him. Jeff disliked school when he was a child and never, ever did his homework. He tolerated endless rebukes and occasional detentions, from which he escaped as soon as he could, to run home and take refuge in his bedroom with his art materials and sketch books.

He grinned. "Yeah. Just in scribbles!" There was a weary look in his blue eyes but he kept on smiling at his sister. Bravely, he continued to plan. When he returned to the flat, he would call her and she could visit; even stay over! They would open a bottle of wine ... He pondered for a moment and remembered her favourite. *Pinot Grigio*. He would show her his manuscript so that she could proofread it and check the spelling; after that, they would talk all night.

Jeff reached for a cup and tried to take a sip of milk but he could barely swallow. He coughed. Unable to help him, Sarah twisted the tissues in her fingers, wishing she could give him some of her own vitality. She was lightly suntanned and healthy after days spent in her garden during an especially warm springtime. It seemed truly bizarre for her to be vibrant when he was so weak. Quietly, she stayed beside her brother, smoothing invisible creases in crisp white sheets until her nervousness eased.

They talked or shared peaceable silences for a couple of hours. No one interrupted their time together. In a couple of beds nearby, patients slept on. A window above Sarah's head was open and a breath of fresh air was cool and welcome. Jeff gazed past her, at mown lawns and flower beds bright with pink-and-white begonias and yellow daisies, which could be seen through the spotless glass doors beside him. Squirrels played there, he told Sarah, and a mallard duck sometimes marched by, with a brood of identical little ones following her.

Sarah didn't talk about her ex-husband and the scandal of his disappearance with their shared savings. She had moved on, was no longer upset, and there was no need to worry Jeff with the details. Instead, she spoke about her daughter, Celeste. He listened with interest; he had been out-of-touch with the family for a long time. In turn, he confided a few mildly shocking things about events on his travels. A few times, he closed his eyes and drifted into sleep for some minutes, affected by the steady dose of morphine dripping into his left arm.

"After I go back to the flat," he began again, forgetting they had already discussed it. "I will call you!"

Jeff slept, then stirred and a nurse came to his side to support him on his way to the toilet. Again, Sarah longed to help somehow; he stood with difficulty and the drip stand had to be wheeled along beside him. The sight of his thin limbs and faltering movements made her heart ache. In his mid-forties, he was still a young man.

She was thankful that she knew about Jeff's return from abroad, and his illness. On admission to the hospice, he had been asked for contact numbers. He must have saved telephone numbers somehow, or remembered postcodes, and a persistent member of staff in administration had managed to speak to Sarah herself, and her sisters, the twins.

Patiently, she waited for the nurse to escort her brother back to his bed. She gathered her possessions before kissing him again, where he lay tucked neatly beneath the clean linen and a warm blanket.

"I'll go now ... goodbye Jeff," she said, softly. "*I'll see you soon.*"

Sarah forced herself to walk away, past rows of beds with their dozing occupants. When she turned at the door to glance behind her, Jeff was watching and, somehow, she forced herself to smile.

She saw him mouth two words. "*Love you!*"

* * *

Two days later, Sarah received a telephone call from a nurse, with the message that Jeff was very unwell. She returned to the hospice, where her brother's bed had been wheeled into a side ward and shielded with floor-length orange-and-white patterned curtains.

To begin with, there was little she could do but be present at the bedside, although she patted her brother's lips and brow with a soft damp cloth and spoke to him reassuringly. Breathing hard, he could not speak but when he felt her hand slip into his, he squeezed it tightly. He kept his eyes closed.

So, Sarah invented small comforts until Jeff began to shift and kick restlessly beneath the bedclothes, becoming increasingly distressed. When he threw his arms above his head and turned his face away with a groan, Sarah stood up and said she would go for help, feeling the situation could surely be eased.

She swished aside the long curtains, crossed the narrow ward and stepped into the corridor. It was moments before she found the nurses' station but there was a pointless delay when she was forced into argument. The young nurse who received Sarah's request looked worried but a second woman, whose head had been bent over paperwork, overheard and came to the front of the desk. She had a brisk manner and a loud voice, and Sarah was immediately annoyed by her behaviour under such sad circumstances.

"We don't *over* medicate," the older nurse said firmly. "It's to make sure the relatives can still talk to them."

Them? Sarah flinched at this awful lack of respect. Jeff's bed was not nearby but she glanced towards the door, which she had left ajar. She knew he had closed his eyes, coping with his suffering; still, she hoped there was no chance that he heard the comment. She took a deep breath and suppressed her anger. In a low tone, she explained she would readily forfeit a chat now, for the sake of

Jeff's comfort.

In the face of her determination, staff called a duty doctor who prepared to obey her request and did not remonstrate. It was difficult to guess how aware Jeff was, he could not speak and the restless movements went on. It was too late to offer him another drink of water, but Sarah tried to comfort him with a gentle hug. She bathed his face and murmured soothing words.

"They're bringing new medicine for you, Jeff! I won't leave."

He was administered with a new drug while she held both his hands in her own, and soon his arms and legs ceased their painful thrashing.

"Well done, Jeff!" The doctor was very kind. She turned to Sarah. "Your brother can hear us. You can talk to him."

Jeff lay quietly at last, and his sister talked, recalling garden games as children, their walks to school in the Essex countryside and trips to the beach in summer. She spoke of Easter treats and Christmas parties, then began to describe her life in the present day. She described her little cat, the cottage garden, her studies and the hopes she cherished for her clever daughter.

Towards the end of the afternoon, Sarah began to watch her brother even more carefully. Was he still drawing breath? His face was impassive, his head lay still and his hand did not grasp hers. Stooping, she thought there was a small rise and fall of his chest. She straightened and stood for a few moments to sip from her water flask. At last, she permitted herself to look away. Through the expanse of crystal-clear glass behind the ward she could see tiny grey squirrels playing. Then, as if the silence deepened, something altered. She turned back to the beloved form in the bed and with a lump in her throat, knowing she had shouldered a burden of responsibility but sure she had been right to ask the doctor to step in, Sarah was able to hold her brother's hand and watch him slip away peacefully, for the sad moment had come.

Two young nurses came softly into the room when Sarah pressed the call switch beside Jeff's bed. There were no loud voices now. They sent her away with instructions to get a cup of tea, and she went to the rest room, where she washed her hands and splashed her face with cool water. She found a vending machine and a toaster beside a loaf of bread on a low table. She selected tea from the machine, drank it from a plastic cup and ate slice of buttered toast. It felt strange to do such small, ordinary things and yet she was hungry and, of course, unhurried. Jeff had passed on and her loving role was over.

By the time she returned to the bedside, the young nurses had tidied the sheets and brushed Jeff's hair. The long ponytail lay smoothly over his shoulder and a posy of flowers had been placed on the white pillow near the handsome face, now shuttered but so dear to his sister. She stood there, with her fingers resting lightly on his sleeve and tears gathering in her eyes.

At last, Sarah had to leave and she kissed her younger brother for one last time. He still looked familiar, she thought. Even so, it was no longer possible to imagine he could wake up.

In the reception room she crossed paths with one of her sisters. Kathy had just turned away from the counter, having spoken to a member of staff and learned she was too late for a final farewell. They murmured a greeting to each other but Sarah saw an expression she recognised on Kathy's face. It was resentment.

A Shock

It was not a cold day but Sarah was shivering. She took a folded blanket from behind a chair cushion, shook it out and pulled the chair close to the fireplace. She lit a match and held it to newspaper and kindling in the grate, then had to light another as her hand shook and the flame was extinguished. Kneeling, she built the fire, adding chunks of coal and a couple of logs collected from a coppice of ash trees behind her cottage. The simple task was an evening ritual which she enjoyed but on this occasion her actions seemed strangely distant from her emotions.

Sarah cast an uneasy glance at a bulky parcel that lay on a table top. Its label bore handwriting she knew well, with the words First Class Post written in thick black letters above the address. Torn open, the parcel had revealed a bundle of documents, and with a warning premonition she had hastily abandoned it.

Now, despite the warmth of her newly crackling fire, Sarah felt a chill. Her heart seemed to beat faster as her breathing quickened. She stood up and reached for the parcel, removed the brown paper and threw it into the fireplace, then sat down, pulled the blanket comfortably over her knees and made efforts to compose herself.

On top of the bulky documents there was a typewritten letter made up of two sheets of paper which had been stapled together.

The text was formatted with double line spacing and much use of capital letters. At first glance, it looked official; however, no company address appeared and some words were misspelt. A good deal of bright yellow highlighting had been applied for emphasis.

The letter began *Dear Sarah* and ended just above a handwritten signature, with *best wishes and love from ...* This turned out to be deeply disingenuous, considering the content.

The sender was Mary, Sarah's older sister, the twin of Kathy. Mary set out details of arrangements for Jeff's funeral. The date, time and order of service with music and readings had all been decided upon; the cost would be almost three-and-a-half thousand pounds and (with the agreement of Kathy) Mary proposed that *Sarah* should pay the bill! It seemed she had discussed the matter with a number of other people and made up her mind about the way in which this was to be done. Sarah was to fill in the form enclosed with her letter and apply for a government grant based on her financial circumstances!

Beneath Mary's signature there was a childish drawing of daisies and an uneven row of scribbled crosses. Sarah stared at these additions. They looked inappropriate and she wondered how anyone would imagine they reduced the brutal shock of a demand for money. The letter was bizarre! Sarah sighed. She turned her attention to the document itself and started to read. She would plough through it. It seemed family members thought they had a good idea, about which she had not been consulted despite their belief in her key role.

Detailed clearly within the first few paragraphs was the fact that *no-one but the organiser of the funeral* may legally make the application. The point was unequivocal. It was so important that it was repeated more than once in the text but Sarah found it leapt into focus immediately. Surely, Mary hadn't read through these pages herself? How did she think her sister could take responsibility?

Please supply information about your relationship to the deceased:

Were you the main carer? (If your answer is no, why are you using this form?)

Were you a full-time carer? (If your answer is no, who shared the caring role? Please supply all their details and contact information.)

Did you share the home of the deceased? (If your answer is no, why not?)

Are you a parent / child / step-child / adopted child of the deceased?

Were you a partner / dependant of the deceased?

What is your marital status?

What is your present address?

What is your present employment? What are the hours you work / income / bank balance?

Detail your savings and monthly outgoings.

Please supply information about all the immediate relatives of the deceased:

List each one and tell us how each relative was involved with the deceased during their lifetime.

Was a relative (not yourself) the main carer? (If your answer is yes, why are you using this form?)

What is each one's marital status / address / employment / hours of work / income / bank balance?

Detail their savings and monthly outgoings.

Please supply information about the deceased:

Did the deceased have a main carer? (If the main carer was not yourself, why are you using this form?)

What was the marital status of the deceased?

What was the address of the deceased before being moved to a hospice?

What was the deceased person's employment (prior to illness) / hours of work / income? What is the deceased person's bank balance?

Did the deceased have an inheritance / any foreign bank accounts or property? Supply details.

Detail their savings.

* * *

The questions were exhausting to read. Mind-blowing, really, thought Sarah! Even if it was appropriate, how would anyone begin to address them all? Precise details were required, including bank reference numbers and each connected person's date of birth. The form was designed for accuracy, in order to ensure there could be no room for error or manipulation of true facts.

When she came to the last page, she was struggling to comprehend that the document had been sent to her. Did Mary think she should try to complete all the complicated details, making her answers fit the questions in an attempt to create a real claim? Or sign the document and return it with a risk of false details being filled in afterwards? There was no question of taking either of those unwise steps, with the high risk of being accused of a fraudulent claim.

Living in a slip of a tumbledown cottage, Sarah had managed on a shoestring since her husband left, some years before. Her daughter was an adult, who returned home for visits but no longer lived there. Working privately as a counsellor, Sarah had improved her situation, built a small nest of savings and had no entitlement to apply to the government for extra money. She could not claim a grant for herself, nor could she apply on behalf of another person.

There was so much to try to comprehend. The twins knew she was not Jeff's carer and hadn't been involved in his life for many years! (Neither, in fact, had they.) Since she was not his parent, child or nurse, nor was she a left-behind partner, Sarah had no right or duty to make a claim now, and yet assumptions must have been made about her personal financial status in order to create a responsibility. Something of a threat seemed implicit in a comment in Mary's letter. *We have signed papers for you!*

Sarah was expected to believe there was no going back, and

refusal to comply might affect some official process already begun. There was attempted force by playing on her emotions and sense of duty. *You are one of the family and everybody is depending on you, Sarah!*

They had speculated shamelessly about her lifestyle and this led to their selection of her, as a target. Sarah was the person who (they thought) must settle their debt. In fact, she could have thrown the unwelcome wad of papers on the fire and she would have been justified.

Common sense and natural intelligence vied with confusion in Sarah's mind. She knew the process had not really begun; it existed in the minds of the twins and that was all. Nevertheless, she wondered what to do. She stayed by the fire with the papers in her hands, until her little black cat came silently to her side and pressed himself against her legs. He was waiting for his tea, and she realised she had been sitting there for a long time. The fire was just a heap of glowing embers and dusk had fallen. She scooped the cat into her arms and pressed her face to his silky head for a moment, then stood up and crossed the darkened room to light a lamp and close the curtains.

There were shopping baskets yet to be unpacked on the kitchen counters but Sarah had forgotten about them. She was experiencing the sense of unreality that comes with a great shock. She transferred the cat from the crook of her arm to the chair, where he purred and treaded cushions while she attended to the fire. Emotional strain affected her physical strength and she felt flat and spiritless with the fight, for the moment, knocked out of her. She dug distractedly at the hot coals and wood with an iron poker until, suddenly flaming again, they released showers of sparks.

Sarah's mood changed. She sat back on her heels and squared her shoulders. "Well now," she remarked aloud. "Sparks *will* fly, if they really think they can treat me like this!" She chose a log from the nearby basket and slung it into the hot coals, sending still more burning fragments flying upwards. She did not cry, although she felt almost childlike again, with startling memories of long-ago taunts from her two sisters. They used to tease and torment Sarah until her thoughts whirled in a storm of anxiety. Fearful and silent, she would bend her head over her story books, often cuddling a kitten in her lap for comfort. Even as a youngster, she knew she didn't deserve to be bullied and would write her thoughts and feelings into a diary which she hid beneath her sweater; a personal record of her unhappiness. The cause of the bullying was a mystery then. It was not until she became an adult and could review all that had happened, that she guessed the twins must have harboured feelings of envy which were hopelessly out of control.

Sarah would have dearly loved to share in the twins' childhood games but she could not, because of their rejection. She was not permitted to raise her voice to the pair, or argue for her right to join in, a situation which led her to retreat and huddle in the window-seat of the family's sitting room, where she found comfort in reading through stacks of library books. If she chuckled over some funny story, Kathy and Mary laughed at her and sometimes even pushed her, but lashing out in response was never a good idea. Their parents always blamed Sarah for any upset, with stern reproofs. All she could do, was try not to feed their cruelty.

Trying to shake off her unhappy memories, Sarah turned her attention to a few ordinary tasks. She took a kettle to the sink, filled it with water, plugged it into a wall socket and switched it on. Next, she unpacked the shopping bags, hunting for a tin. She opened it, forked the contents into a paw-patterned dish and stooped to offer it to the waiting cat. He received his meal with chirrups of approval but it seemed impossible for Sarah to contemplate preparing food for herself.

She stowed items away in the refrigerator and cupboards, automatically making them tidy, reflecting, as she did so, that there was an uncomfortable conversation ahead. The sisters must be told their plan was not viable.

* * *

Sarah carried a mug of fresh tea to her table, set it down while she found a pencil, then seated herself. She turned again to the form and began to make notes in the margins. It was, in reality, a pointless exercise considering the powerful message on the first page, but a certain fascination gripped her. Again, that sense of distance from reality. The knowledge that her proposed involvement in a fraudulent plan was not going to work, meant she could look dispassionately at the form, treat it logically and prepare her comments for the twins. Nevertheless, it was moments before her feelings crowded in, and she was offended again.

All his bank accounts? Sarah thought, incredulously. *I don't know those details! I wasn't Jeff's partner or carer!*

Being urged to complete and submit a personal claim on behalf of someone else (whose entitlement to the money was nil) made Sarah a victim. It was a harsh truth. It was hard to believe the twins failed to consult her before initiating a course of action that could send them all to court if she tried to comply. They would get into trouble for deception! This uncomfortable situation was all the more painful in that it must have been planned.

Sarah frowned over the pages and wrote her notes until, for the time being, she had exhausted her thoughts. She straightened the documents on the table, then went to the fireplace and covered it safely with a wire guard. Moving quietly, she mounted a narrow staircase, heading for the bathroom. Nervous shivers had stopped. She felt hot with the emotions that couldn't be denied and her reflection in the mirror showed wide eyes, a shocked expression and fair hair falling loosely around her cheeks, where spots of high colour burned. She filled the basin and washed in cool water, then held her wet hands over her face, fingers splayed, breathing in the refreshing fragrance of lemon soap.

"Do something!" She told her mirror image. She ducked her head, rinsed away bubbles and reached for a towel. Barefoot on the soft, pale carpet of the upstairs landing, still patting her skin dry, she made her way to her bedroom door before remembering that her mobile phone was out of charge. Turning around, she headed for the telephone in her narrow hallway.

Sarah was resolute as she keyed in Mary's number. For sure, there was no need to try to fill in and sign the form! Still, she was to regret calling with an explanation, which she intended for the benefit of both sisters. With Mary's angry response it was impossible to avoid an argument and later, despairing over the cost to her peace of mind, she reflected that she should have simply carried on as normal, countering any incoming calls with a calm recommendation of legal advice.

Clutching the telephone in one hand and her hand towel in the other, she sat on the lower step of the cottage staircase and struggled with another shock, for her sensible comments met with fury and her honest efforts to explain further were declared "distorted".

FRIENDS

Mary had provided her sister with a document which was obviously designed for completion by a person whose links and involvement with the deceased were practical and comprehensive during his lifetime. Sarah had misgivings as soon as she saw it and they worsened upon reading it for the first time. However, to try to gain an understanding of Mary's viewpoint, she checked every page carefully, hunting for any detail that could make her first impression questionable. Her endeavour felt foolish because of the immediate warning about the appropriate claimant. This must be the person who dealt with the funeral arrangements, so there was no question of pretending Sarah was that person, or that she could act as if it were true. Still, she tried to be open to a different view in the interests of avoiding a family dispute.

It wasn't possible to share Mary's stance. One would need to undertake a great deal of work to investigate and fully detail the financial status of every member of her brother's family and, since Sarah had no right to take on the claim, none of it would be worth it!

The next day, equipped with the best understanding she could achieve, Sarah reviewed the situation overall. She felt deepening alarm. Its enormity became evident in terms of gossip and false perceptions of herself. Points she skimmed past at first, took on more significance. What conversations had she shared in the past, that led the sisters to imagine she would remain in receipt of benefits even while she was in work? Why did they think she had access to a support system, or that it could genuinely be spread over her wider family? They were not in contact with her often, but that should have been an extra reason for them to be careful.

The whole thing was silly, Sarah thought. Moreover, the implications of the sisters' perceptions made her feel embarrassed and angry. She asked a couple of trusted friends to give her an honest opinion, calling them one at a time to outline her situation.

"I can't get my breath!" Carla marvelled, after listening attentively to a description of events. Carla was a journalist and she was used to writing about cases of slander and libel. "They've been discussing your money? For goodness' sake, that's not allowed! Sarah, people probably won't believe them, though. I think you should take no notice of them." Struck by a thought, she went on. "Why would Mary want to take over the whole situation?"

There was a pause. Sarah knew the answer to this question but her mind suddenly filled with memories. Mary had been deliberately controlling for years. Kathy loved to back her up.

"I was with Jeff when he passed away," she faltered, getting a lump in her throat. "They were too late. They don't like it when I seem to play a part in family life; they never did. I should probably take no notice of them, although ... I don't know if they will go away!"

Another friend was a barrister-at-law. During shared studies in psychology, Glynis had spotted that Sarah possessed a logical mind and was inclined to persuade her to study law, too. Despite her learned status, her first comment was brief. "They've gone mad!"

Sarah smiled, despite her unhappiness. "They have always seen things very differently from the way I do!"

"*Differently?*" Glynis exclaimed. "Crookedly, I'd say! Are they drinking?" She began to laugh but she was not as flippant as she seemed. "Sarah, this could run you into real problems, so you mustn't allow yourself to be coerced! I'm sure you won't. Trying to go along with it would be fraudulent; you could end up in a publicised legal case against you and lose credibility in your work. Throw every single one of those papers away!"

It was helpful to know her friends saw the disgraceful injustice in events. They knew she was not being treated fairly, or lawfully. *Take no notice … throw away the papers!* These were forceful messages from two clever women who took similar viewpoints to one another. Sarah respected them but, even so, it was oddly difficult to decide to cast aside the form and still harder to stop troubled thoughts from darting about in turmoil. The fact was, Sarah was so badly shaken that common sense vied with a feeling of sheer panic.

At length, in a compromise of sorts, she folded Mary's letter, tucked it inside the document, made the whole bundle into a tightly taped parcel and (feeling faintly ridiculous) hid everything beneath her bed! "So, it's out of sight and out of mind, for now!" She observed, although she spoke only to the watching cat.

Even while she reassured herself, Sarah knew she still struggled with confusion. When someone's actions are pointless, no matter how strong the case for discarding all thoughts surrounding them, they may not be negligible. They can have an effect. If the culprit is determined, harm can still be done. Sarah's thoughts *were* affected; she began to be plagued by guilt and the anxiety wouldn't leave. She was in danger of becoming unwell from stress.

Mary and Kathy hurled themselves at their attempts to force her hand and the level of distress they caused was very high. Before long, Sarah realised, if strangers did the same, she would be wise to involve the police! When the telephone rang, she jumped. They tried to prolong conversations, although she patiently reminded them that facts must not be altered to fit the requirements of their form. Knowing she was correct, was no protection from her sense of upset.

Sarah decided to ask for an opinion from someone with relevant knowledge. Her friends had been supportive but an impartial view could help.

* * *

The young man at the advisory bureau was pleasant but hurried. Waiting behind Sarah was a queue of people who wanted to talk about government benefits and housing problems. She explained her concerns as concisely as she could but her heart sank fast. He wouldn't meet her eyes. It seemed he couldn't see a role in advising Sarah, even though much of his work related to the strict rules and regulations of the benefits system. Perhaps he simply couldn't be bothered? The form, along with her situation, must have looked complicated.

Sarah had smoothed her hair into a fair, glossy ponytail. She wore a neat, fawn cape and carried a roomy leather handbag. She didn't look needy in comparison with many claimants who regularly flooded into the offices of the support service.

"Well, you know, this is only a disagreement about a form!" The man glanced past her, towards the door. He was probably hoping for a more straightforward customer. "Perhaps you should just fill it in?"

A Beautiful Life

Sarah's parents owned a thatched cottage on the outskirts of a country town and in some ways their children's lives were free, with lots of opportunities to be happy. There were mossy lawns to play on, fruit trees that could be climbed and used as vantage points to look across the other gardens nearby, and masses of flowers in broad, well-tended beds or spilling from wooden planters. A heavy gate headed the wide driveway and the children loved to hang over it, to swing. Beyond the long back garden there was woodland; further still, were fields where bales of straw were turned into dens in August and September, young heifers grazed all summer and wildlife was abundant.

The children were given toys and birthday parties, and there were no strict rules of behaviour in their household. They ate home-cooked food of which there was plenty, always vegetarian and somewhat heavy on rice dishes. There was chocolate at Easter and (except for roast turkey) the proper festive foods and traditions at Christmas. In summer, the family spent days by the sea. In winter, there were walks and games in the snow.

It was a framework in which contentment should have been theirs, a given right of little children. However, their parents, Lena and Eddie, shared a certain careless disinterest in them as individuals and this could affect them adversely.

Jeff almost drowned when he was a toddler, having strayed into the deep part of a swimming-pool while Lena drank coffee and chatted with friends. He was rescued when two young women spotted him sinking and they brought him, dripping and yelling, to Lena. After they handed him over, she wrapped her small son in a towel and held him on her lap for a few minutes. The child quietened down and the other women were quiet too, not knowing what to say given the mother's oddly calm response to the drama.

"They were cross, weren't they?" Lena commented, referring to the young rescuers without obvious embarrassment or concern.

The children were collected in a mini-bus, which travelled a mile to a tiny primary school each day. They were supervised on the trip by a pleasant older lady, who sat behind the driver. She was there to help children to board and leave the bus with their bags. It was an arrangement that might have been full of fun but both Sarah and Jeff were transported unhappily; they didn't want to go.

Difficulties in education such as Sarah's mental block about mathematics and resulting anxiety during lessons and tests, were never addressed. Jeff was painfully shy and, without the help he needed, he became introverted and silent in school Their father, who was academic, could not contemplate his family being any less able than he was; options such as arranging extra tuition or even supplying help and advice himself were unthinkable, while their mother merely assumed, because they were sent regularly to school, she fulfilled her duty.

In fact, the children were not encouraged to report back to their parents with their childish perceptions of any life experience. Dental treatment was miserable for they were made to visit a harsh, unsympathetic practitioner and neither Lena nor Eddie thought to enter the surgery to oversee procedures. Unaware that they should have been accompanied and treated kindly, Sarah, Jeff and the twins emerged with pale faces and tearful voices after each appointment, but their distress went unremarked.

Youngsters know only what their own experience offers them; the children were used to being treated carelessly and it was a time when kind practitioners with special measures in place to comfort youngsters were rare. In a situation where more discerning parents would have seen how shocked they were, nothing removed them from the painful, damaging episodes they were undergoing and they could not complain.

* * *

When he was very young, Jeff was often dressed in oversized clothes which had been handed down from a cousin. He was a pretty child, with a forelock of fair hair that fell into his wide blue eyes and an engaging grin. However, his nature was sensitive; he wept easily and his parents made no secret of the fact that they saw this as a failing.

Eddie seemed unable to empathise with this child who was different in character and abilities from himself and he developed a habit of insulting his son from an early age. He was irritated by Jeff's love of art and sometimes ridiculed his efforts; perhaps he was unintentionally harsh but, with confidence eroded, the child learned to hide his drawings.

Lena was dismissive of Jeff's tears. She was inclined to call him silly and the unkindness of both parents led to his inability to work well in school, since he knew he would not be praised. Growing older, he always drew and painted but he always hid his pictures.

Inevitably, Jeff had a tough time in school. His father was too lofty to discuss his children with teachers and his mother was unreceptive to descriptions of troubles in class but, at the tiny primary school during the nineteen-sixties, parents' evenings were never held and disinterested families were not identified. They were not required to engage in their children's education.

By the time he was sixteen years old, Jeff was out of school with no plans to return for the sixth form. He was a troubled young man who had no safe, older person to turn to with his deep-rooted sense of unease. He was paid scant attention. In keeping with his gentle soul, once he decided enough was enough, he caused no fuss but quietly packed up his sketchbooks, pencils and brushes, along with an armful of clothes, biscuits from the kitchen pantry and a tiny amount of money saved from a paper round. He stuffed everything into a worn backpack and left home. A note was found on his untidy single bed, with just a few lines to explain his intention to travel far away and that was what he did, picking up casual jobs here and there, living from hand-to-mouth. Before long, he was not in contact with his parents at all and they had no idea of his where-abouts, his state of health or his income.

Lena did not seem concerned for Jeff's safety. Incredibly, she con-tinued to seem contented, as if her life was agreeable; her mind untroubled. Perhaps it was easier to choose not to worry. In assum-ing that her young son was equipped to look after himself, she didn't suffer torment. She must have been oblivious to the possibil-ity of blaming herself for his absence.

CHILDHOOD

After a traumatic experience of childbirth when she needed an unplanned Caesarean section, Sarah was thrilled with her tiny daughter but found she couldn't stop herself from sliding into depression. She had hoped for a home delivery and envisaged a peaceful start to her child's life. With the sudden urgency of the operation followed by lingering emotional shock and some physical discomfort afterwards, she felt unhappy.

During this time of feeling depressed, the task of caring for baby Celeste felt overwhelming on top of other daily duties. Sarah knew, logically, she could come forward from the experience of giving birth but she became very tired. Determined to breastfeed her child, she gathered information from a health visitor and a library book, and made her way through the early worries about the quantity and quality of her milk; a mildly irritating tendency in herself to forget which breast she needed to offer at each feed, and a seriously uncomfortable episode of blocked milk ducts. Her husband was unhelpful and frequently absent from home. She put his absences down to the pressure of work at the time but he persistently left her alone. He would return, insisting he still loved Sarah and his child but his behaviour made her suspicious; she thought there could be another woman in his life.

There were times when Sarah's life felt bleak. It would have been a relief to lean on a loving mother but Lena was dismissive of her illness. She seemed determined that it would disappear if Sarah would only adopt a more positive attitude. It was careless treatment which highlighted the fact that Lena probably never had much empathy with her youngest daughter. Despite Sarah's best efforts to be positive, she found herself dwelling on memories, even obsessing about the reasons for unhappy family relationships in a train of thought which made her fight with depression all the harder.

* * *

There were episodes of neglect during her childhood and Sarah could never discern any good reason for them. If a handful of accidents and misadventures are an inevitable part of childhood, it is certainly a parent's duty to deal with them properly and yet, while her mother seemed committed to her family, there were some worrying events.

The children played in the fields and woodland surrounding the cottage, spending hours making dens or climbing trees, happy but unsupervised. When a fall from a tree resulted in concussion for Sarah, she was put into her bed with typical careless haste and left there, lying alone for some hours. The feckless parents were persuaded to call for an ambulance only after a neighbour happened to call in and learned of the accident from the chatter of the other children. She asked to visit the little girl and was shown into the bedroom.

"She's just bumped her head!" Lena said, unconcerned. "She'll sleep it off!"

Sarah wasn't asleep. Kind Mrs Taylor saw the child's listless, confused condition and encouraged the family to seek urgent medical care.

* * *

Sarah's gentle demeanour and quaint prettiness gained her friends who responded to her air of fragility and often tried to mother her.

When she was ten years old, a classmate wanted to tidy her long fair hair but was shocked when she loosened the braids and made efforts to release them. Embarrassingly for both the youngsters, the comb caught in thick matts and tangles. At home, Sarah described her friend's astonishment with innocent candour but her mother's response was not to take her daughter to a salon to rectify the situation. Instead, she scrabbled in a drawer for kitchen scissors and cut Sarah's hair into a boyish crop, an action that dismayed the child and drew further bullying from classmates the next day.

Eddie's income was substantial, which made it possible for Lena to avoid going out to work and the couple employed an elderly gentleman to tend the gardens and take care of odd jobs around the house too. Lena was cushioned from many difficulties. Somewhat fey, she daydreamed her way through an existence that allowed her to be self-indulgent. She grew flowers, tackled light housework and cooked the foods she enjoyed. She read magazines and romantic novels. Her eyes were not open to the potential for suffering that lies in a neglected child.

Sarah liked to sit near the kindly gardener as he stooped over his spade or planted seedlings. Sprawling on a rug with her books and kittens in her lap, she offered her confidences, knowing he listened and would not rebuke her. When the old man suddenly died, she was informed casually from across the room upon her return from school that evening. She had been comforted by her friend and had even become dependent upon him, in a way. Sarah had learned not to make a fuss but the loss was a cruel blow.

Fairly frequently, she was sent to stay for several days at a time with her grandmother. It was an arrangement which seemed to suit Lena and, fortunately, the child was happy to go along with it, too. Removed from most of her possessions and her pets, Sarah was sometimes bored but she always took her favourite story books and a bundle of sketch pads and pencils. At least she was not bullied. Grandma was a stout lady, who wore her short grey hair tightly permed. Generally dressed in an enveloping pinafore, she was some-what dour but fundamentally good-natured. Occasionally she placed a box of new paints, or a treat such as a bar of chocolate, beside Sarah's nicely-made bed.

Like her favourite kitten at home, a little cat provided affection-ate company in Grandma's house. He was an elderly ginger tabby, who turned up at the door one day, was fed scraps from the table, begged again the following day and then often returned throughout one summer. When cold weather arrived and he continued to look for food, a bed was made for him in a cardboard box which was soon shifted from the wood shed into the kitchen near the warmth of the old Aga. He stayed, grew plump and was called, simply, "Ginger".

Her pets were the recipients of many childish confidences but when something made Sarah cry, she hid in the bathroom. After the tears had stopped, she dabbed white talcum powder on her cheeks to try to reduce flushing before emerging to seek comfort, quietly, in her books and drawings. In a similar way to her small brother, she had to conceal any upset lest bullying intensified, so that her true character and abilities were blanketed, with much that should have been praised, in fact, sadly overlooked.

Sarah was a fragile child who could never eat a large meal. Being faced with a plate heaped with food made her feel reluctant to touch any of it. When Eddie made a reference to this over the din-ner table one Sunday she sat in silence and no-one around the table noticed or cared that she was then unable to take another mouthful. In primary school, when a lunchtime assistant called her a "slow eater" the child thought it was an ailment and was frightened. At the age of eleven, she won a scholarship which led to her being sent to an all-girls grammar school, where she immediately felt insig-nificant and terribly shy. Primary education in a tiny church school had not prepared her for corridors, crowds or strict routines with disciplinary measures a constant threat. She was hopelessly intimidated by stern teachers and confident classmates, many of whom received extra coaching from private tutors in order to bring their work to a high standard.

Sarah didn't understand the grammar school system and had no idea what to do about her fright. Wearing a dark blue overall, she had to stand alongside other students at a long bench, to learn about the Bunsen burner. She scorched a fingertip, couldn't understand the teacher's instructions or make sense of the printed instruction sheet, felt overwhelmed and hated everything about the process. At home, she urgently needed to confide the details of her new school life and her struggle to adjust to an environment she found hateful from the start. She longed to ask questions and gain support, so that she didn't accidentally break a set of strict rules never before encountered. Casual parenting, however, left aside any kindly interest and neither Eddie nor Lena wanted to know how their daughter was faring. They could certainly afford to pay a tutor for private additional lessons but they were contemptuous of parents who saw the need. Even though she was very young, Sarah knew this after she overheard a comment about a friend's child.

At the end of the first week, Sarah hesitated on the doorstep before leaving the house in the morning. She was uncomfortable, dressed in a navy-blue uniform with an obligatory red beret which was dreadfully hard to keep on her head. In her hand she held a briefcase, purchased on some whim by Eddie. Sarah would have dearly loved a soft leather satchel, to sling casually over one shoulder and make her feel the same as the other girls! She felt ridiculous when she held the narrow handle of the case, which seemed to drag her down.

"Oh!" she said, painfully. "I don't want to go!"

It was an uncharacteristic protest and Lena should have been alarmed. Instead, keeping her back turned, she twisted a tap and reached for a plastic bottle of dishwashing liquid. With the sound of water hitting the stone sink, she plunged her hands into foam and began to scrub crockery. "You have to!" She would not acknowledge her daughter's desperation.

Sarah was far too timid to run back into the house. She was forced to head for the chilly bus stop, the lonely, jerking ride and the intimidating atmosphere of the school she hated so much.

After that, Sarah did not know how to ask for help to cope with the harshness of the grammar school environment. Her suffering was acute and it was ongoing. She became withdrawn, remained largely silent in school, and was often overlooked for some small achievement for which others gained a reward. This disregard, as if she was invisible because of her timidity, included her efforts to walk smartly into morning assembly. Sarah always made sure to walk upright to the best of her ability. Nevertheless, she had to watch the more extrovert girls receive the coveted deportment badge. Some lucky classmates even decorated a whole lapel on their blazers with the bright red badges but Sarah never got a single one, although she deserved it!

Perhaps her natural reserve meant she was not equipped to cope in the more relaxed atmosphere of a comprehensive school? There, the potential for more noise and bustle was the result of fewer rules. It was just possible her parents thought so, but there was never a conversation on the subject and it was far more likely they ignored signs of distress. A school where there was less emphasis on achieving perfection might have eased Sarah's fears, a new group of friends might have taken her sweet nature to their hearts, and some aspects of her loneliness could have ended.

In later years, Sarah occasionally let her memory linger over the truth about her schooldays. Her parents failed her, neglecting their responsibilities. Throughout the years of her secondary school education, she was not protected. She was never given the opportunity to change.

The twins were not intimidated by school rules or power-crazed teachers. They were not fearful and they stolidly resisted attempts to encourage high performance in obligatory examinations. They did not try particularly hard to pass tests and so they were both spared the ordeal of the excessive demands of a grammar school. Perhaps that was to their liking. They always had one another for support. Nevertheless, the difference between their attitudes and experiences could have been a fundamental cause of their perception of a distance between themselves and Sarah. They had made their choices and yet their resentment became intense after she stopped following in their footsteps. She was the only one to be sent to a girls' grammar school.

Bullying behaviour from the older twins was extreme in childhood and it was beyond Sarah's comprehension then, but possible causes became clearer when her mind returned to it in later years. There had been a good deal of proud boasting from Eddie, who didn't conceal his love of academic success. He was pleased when Sarah passed examinations, and this made Mary and Kathy jealous. They seemed to have no protective instincts towards their younger sister; they were not sympathetic or interested enough to learn that she was frightened, hated school and took no pleasure in wearing layers of dull, loose-fitting clothes or trying, pointlessly, to keep a flat, red beret on her head.

Eddie simply could not understand that his children differed from himself. Yet, how odd: the twins were not in line for his criticism while Sarah could never get anything right. If she was good at English, why was she not good at Maths? Eddie said, this didn't make sense. If she was sad, he only became harsh. Was he afraid of her sadness?

Neither parent could face the reality of their children's emotions. Perhaps, since the twins showed scant evidence of tender feelings and were not ridiculed, aspects of neglect didn't matter to them. Sarah and Jeff were artistic, sensitive souls and they were made to suffer.

"Bothering Sarah" became a regular, unkind game but no adult ever wondered why the gentle girl, with her nerves tested to the limit, occasionally risked reproach to turn angrily on the twins. Sarah couldn't express her misery in school or explain to her family that she truly detested feeling different, so they taunted her freely until they tired of it and ran away, leaving her still trying to read stories despite her spinning thoughts.

* * *

Transference
Sometimes, people carry forward childish patterns of behaviour into their adult lives. For instance, if a fit of weeping was once a sure way to bring about a change of heart from a strict father, a woman might adopt the same behaviour to make it difficult for a partner to disagree in an adult relationship. She may not be thinking the process through, not consciously and yet when someone whom she loves (and expects to give love in return) does not see things her way, tears will come and the hope of creating guilt and a change of heart is there.

As life goes on, an individual has a certain unconscious expectation of similarity in each new relationship and often they try to recreate that familiar framework even if it didn't feel as if it worked well, before. Where early experiences were satisfactory, this may lead to readiness to be honest and assertions of affection, but if a personal history was less than perfect, the process of forming a bond with a new partner can cause unhappiness all over again. Deep-rooted memories of the cause and effects of past trauma can mean responses in the present are identical to those that once presented long ago, often to the astonishment of the recipient of emotional affects (in the Freudian sense) such as anger or an accusation based on an apparently unreasonable sense of insult.

The Twins
When the twins were born, as so often happens, the first baby to be

delivered was a satisfactory weight and looked strong and healthy, while the second was smaller and gave the attending midwives some cause for concern. Kathy was delicate and Lena was advised to keep this in mind. During the early weeks following the birth, a health visitor made sure to check on the mother and her twins at regular intervals.

Lena obeyed instructions and Kathy was cosseted. She was fed on demand, in the natural way which brings news infants forward safely and well. Also, she received prescribed extra vitamins. As time went on, a continued effort was maintained to ensure she ate well. She grew, caught up with her twin and became sturdy. Kathy had been favoured, in a way, by parents who were normally somewhat cool and whose children lacked some of the comfort and kindness which more obviously loving families demonstrate naturally. Effects lingered but she was not spiritual. She developed a blustering desire for attention and a certain intolerance of hardship.

Fractionally senior by a few minutes, Mary was strong when she was young. Non-identical to her twin, she looked similar in adulthood nevertheless, especially when the pair shopped for clothes together and shared trips to the hairdresser's salon, where they got their hair dyed a hard, reddish colour. Both women were judgemental, so confident their churchgoing habit made them excellent citizens that they never considered being in the wrong. Each of them was cushioned by a husband who could afford a comfortable life, and resources of courage and emotional intelligence were not tested, although the cruel loss of their mother brought some new awareness of the human side of life.

They indulged themselves, acquiring masses of possessions without which their lives might have been equally comfortable. Their extravagant lifestyle included frequent holidays and lavish parties. They couched most of their responses, no matter what happened, in wine, treats and loud laughter.

The twins were used to being free to upset their sister during their younger years and maturity had not made them review their behaviour. They formed a gang of two when they were jealous of Sarah and her high school life, and sadly they could stop her from telling their parents because she was afraid of being scolded. The only time she tried to ask Lena directly to put a stop to the taunts, there was a curt response. Sarah herself was at fault, the mother said. Whatever it was she had done to annoy them, she must stop getting in their way.

The twins' expectations were always that they could manipulate Sarah in any situation. In adulthood, they continued to believe Sarah was without the right or power to protest.

Counter Transference

The recipient of a certain approach may unconsciously accept his or her role, so that a pattern of behaviour emerges because it's expected of them.

In the weeping child adult scenario, the father once capitulated and comforted her. Now the partner may feel guilty and give in. Her tears make the partner feel like the one in the wrong, because that is exactly her expectation.

For Sarah, there was a certain awareness that the two older women had never altered but that she, herself, need not fall back into old ways. Holding out against them was surprisingly difficult because she had often felt intimidated when she was young. When the twins expected to force her hand, the same feelings were renewed. Flooding back, came memories of her forlorn hope that her mother would end the bullying, along with the fact that Lena chose not to step in.

Sarah listened to friends whom she respected. They expressed disgust (*I can't get my breath!*) and even ridicule (*are they drinking?*) and they both advised her to discard the muddle of instructions she had received. Ignore the twins … fling the form away and forget it … yet, she could not. That sense of being in the wrong was there;

the parents had reinforced it with their failures and neglect. She never received comfort from them and it was hard to find a safety net in a new, similar scenario.

ADULTS

There was a time when the three sisters were peaceable. They all became mothers for the first time during one year, when new experiences and the shared interest of caring for their babies drew them together more happily than ever before. Kathy was not as deliberately competitive as Mary and she could spend time with Sarah, simply enjoying the fun their youngsters brought them. Their mother loved parties and despite her failure to make emotional connections with her children, she enjoyed creating family gatherings.

Lena provided baskets full of toys and heaped the table with good food, allowing the little cousins to enjoy each other's company with family resentments hidden and old hurts in the background. Sarah was wise enough to know that disagreements happen in many families and she genuinely hoped for a sustained change.

The thread of rejection was not completely gone and it resurfaced eventually although, like many victims, Sarah only wished for ill-treatment to end; she had no interest in winning arguments which she never deliberately initiated. She often learned of her exclusion from some activity which the twins' families shared, despite the fact that Sarah and her daughter would have loved to join in. As her life progressed, her history of abuse sometimes played on her mind. She confronted disturbing memories during her counselling training, especially in the study of psychodynamic theories.

Poor Lena died before her sixtieth birthday, following a foolish misdiagnosis from a local doctor who told her he thought her persistent pain was caused by irritable bowel disorder. This piece of catastrophic misinformation was handed to Lena without the benefit of clinical tests but she was of a generation that firmly believes in the wisdom of the family practitioner and she didn't think it was necessary to challenge her doctor, or ask for a second opinion. By the time her symptoms worsened, it was too late for medical help to save her.

Family dynamics altered and it became more difficult to share contented times. Sarah felt deeply saddened and angered to think a life could be cut short without proper help, affected by the careless disinterest of a trusted medical person. Perhaps the depth of her grief came unexpectedly, with its sickening early effects and the gradual change to life without Lena, when (as all bereaved people must) she found that one can both experience sadness and carry on in life. Sarah was certainly acutely aware of hurtful memories but she missed the physical grace of her mother and that fey presence which was often so carefree, even in the face of her child's misery.

Never obviously loving, Lena was always in trouble if her emotions were called into question or if she was called upon to provide emotional support for her children. Yet, surely there was the expression of love in many of her actions. She had created a beautiful environment and was essentially committed to many aspects of maintaining the family. Perhaps her great failure was in missing the fact that each of her children was a different individual. She simply couldn't reach out to each one, separately.

* * *

After the early passing of Lena, poor Eddie couldn't bear his loneliness. He remarried hastily, having sought a companion while he was still stricken by grief. A local woman whom he barely knew was happy to accept his offer but there was an ulterior motive at the root of her interest.

Once she was safely married, Noelle made excuses not to leave her own house at once and after just a few months when she visited but rarely stayed a night in Eddie's house and never took an interest in making it feel homelike, she left him and disappeared from the village. She wrote letters, telling Eddie she prayed she could remain his wife. She would come back, she promised; she just needed to get her thoughts straight. Everyone except Eddie knew she was keeping her options open but he waited. In reality, it was as if the brief relationship never happened but in his state of denial, he did not divorce Noelle. He would not discuss her with his daughters and precious savings, which had accumulated during his first marriage, became the woman's property after he eventually passed away.

Before that, he was reclusive, seeming to seek the solitary life he had feared, keeping to simple daily rituals with times he would not vary for meals, baths and sleep. He depended upon the television for entertainment. He had lost interest in reading and research, although he received invitations to join former friends and colleagues and would have been capable of delivering seminars at the local university, or conducting after-dinner speeches. He was impossible to help as he sank, too soon, into the habits of an old man. Inevitably, he began to be left alone; his world narrowed and time was spent in front of his favourite programmes, except for excursions into the kitchen or bathroom. He ate microwaved meals directly from plastic trays and seemed to prefer to be alone, despite occasionally complaining about it.

Depressed and idle, Eddie took no interest in sorting out Lena's possessions and Sarah was reluctant to force him to do it but when she eventually looked for bundles of diaries, cookery books and familiar novels. as well as jewellery, her search was in vain. A set of beautiful crockery was missing, along with many other items. It seemed that Sarah had left her investigations into the attic and spare rooms too late. Eddie did not mention his deceased wife's private diaries and when Sarah risked delicate questions, he professed no knowledge of the whereabouts of her belongings.

It was not until Jeff passed away and new events shed light on the old, that Sarah realised what must have happened. The unscrupulous Noelle was disinterested in anything except Eddie's legacy but when it came to items, the twins had not stood back.

During her studies in psychology, Sarah learned that a bereaved man might try to replace his lost partner very fast or retreat from the world, shedding many old habits and values. In the end, poor Eddie did both.

THE WHIRLWIND

Throughout the week following Jeff's passing the old sensation of being helplessly caught up in a storm of confusion made Sarah's head spin. Inevitably, she remembered only too well that unreal world, where she had done nothing wrong but was made to feel the opposite was true.

In an effort to bring some sort of order into the ideas the twins must have been fostering together, Sarah spoke to Kathy on the telephone and suggested a meeting. It was obvious there would be difficulties in arranging a funeral, since Jeff himself had almost certainly left no provision for its costs; also, she felt worried about the possessions that lay abandoned in the flat in London.

To begin with, Kathy was agreeable and even seemed glad to make some plans with her sister. Relieved, Sarah contacted Mary. Unfortunately, even though she was asked to join in, Mary was irritated. She told Sarah to cancel the meeting, insisting she was too busy and therefore they must wait. Concerned, Sarah began to argue her point about delays. Mary angrily accused her of being insensitive.

Perhaps she was being too hasty? Sarah thought. Neither Kathy nor Mary had been able to say a proper farewell to their brother. Maybe she *was* treading on their toes, with her sense of urgency? The immediate shock of their loss could take some days to ease, and

Sarah was acutely aware that sorrow would linger afterwards, of course. She left the pair alone, only to learn that they met one another within twenty-four hours of her conversation with Mary, at which time, regardless of options, they booked a meeting with an undertaker of Mary's choosing.

Mary seemed to have appointed herself executor of the estate, such as it was. However, she did not speak to Sarah about entitlement and would not apply for a grant of representation.

The ferocity of the argument Sarah encountered each time she tried to communicate with her sisters, was alarming. She realised she was deliberately excluded from decision-making and was incredulous. As a counsellor she had chosen to train specifically in key aspects of loss and bereavement; she had relevant knowledge about procedure and much to offer. Regardless of this, she was treated dismissively. Before long, the old enmity was there and it was a dreadful block to common sense.

Kathy adopted her favourite habit of supporting anything Mary wanted to say or do, regardless of whether or not she seemed to be following a wise course of action. Mary, she said, would take care of everything.

"It's not a competition, you know!" Kathy remarked, rudely. "You just seem to want to fight us, Sarah!"

By this time, Sarah was coping with intense annoyance but she tried to keep calm and strong. There was nothing to be gained by shouting or becoming upset and there was still so much to do, to honour their brother and lay him to rest in an appropriate way. She explained their sister ought not to assume responsibility without mutual agreement but her words fell on deaf ears. Kathy refused to consider the idea of properly shared responsibility, or the possibility of a discussion to reach agreement between all three women. In fact, it was hard, she said (apparently rejecting the very fact that Sarah spoke at all), to believe anyone could be so nasty and selfish at this dreadful time! All this was making her feel ill, Kathy declared. She would get worse, if they had to keep talking.

The twins were not open to a discussion of the type of funeral to suit the circumstances. Dismayed, Sarah saw that Mary considered herself above lawful processes and Kathy colluded with this delusional belief. On the subject of legal advice, they thought Mary's occasional voluntary assistance in a charity shop supplied her with acquaintances who had relevant experience! They were determined that this was satisfactory and that there was no need for the services of a qualified solicitor. On behalf of the charity, Mary often received bundles from house clearances when someone had passed away. In the course of her helpful work, she talked to all sorts of bereaved people and she was perfectly well-informed as a result. She had all the expertise they needed, said the sisters.

Sarah found she could not break free from her worries. When people try to address a serious matter without the benefit of the skills which experts train for years to acquire, often their ignorance can lead to disaster. Trying to think of the very best ways to help, she wrote emails, labouring over the wording. Her messages immediately met with ridicule and it was obvious the content was not really understood.

After a few days, the twins must have decided they could access their sister's money and their approach altered. She received emphatic messages to say she should attend the meeting at the date and time they chose, to discuss funeral plans with the undertaker. Unaware of her selection as a target for payment, Sarah assumed they had realised they must share the planning and, in a typically straightforward way, she explained she could not contemplate an expensive funeral but she would research entitlements and was happy to meet, minus the presence of a funeral director at this stage since they had private discussion ahead. Perhaps a face-to-face meeting would give Sarah an opportunity to explain their options more effectively? Equipped with her training and experience with clients, she hoped to guide them after all.

Despite her best efforts, or perhaps inevitably (since her ideas were not in line with Mary's) the pair rejected Sarah's offer. Instead, Mary sent a series of text messages to say she would collect her sister in her car and take her to the meeting, which was already booked and must not be altered.

Staying polite somehow, Sarah refused to comply. A sentence formed in her mind. *Don't sign anything!* There seemed to be terrific urgency underlying the twins' actions but it was impossible to introduce a note of caution and the warning words remained unsaid, even though onslaughts on their sister went on. It transpired they planned a holiday for the following week, and they were determined to win the arguments and free themselves in order to go away and relax.

Mary's silly self-aggrandisement was absolute. She sent a furious, reproachful message when she realised Sarah would not fall into line. Kathy copied her, with muddled reminders about family ties.

On Saturday, the postman arrived late in the day. Sarah went to check her mailbox after a shopping trip and found inside a heavy package. It contained a letter as well as dozens of pages of text comprising a complex form with accompanying notes, which had been downloaded from the internet, printed and posted in its entirety to her.

Who was at fault? Sarah began to wonder about the foundation of her sisters' erroneous belief in their form. She guessed they might have received poor advice. Had somebody else been drawn in, with an opportunity to give them false guidance? She took a risk and called Mary.

"No!" Mary answered. "Sarah, what do you think you know? When Lena died, everything was paid for by Eddie. When he passed, there was enough money for that funeral. Then, Noelle got our legacy, so nothing was left for us; but things are different now. I've done a lot of charity work since then; there are ways to bring in some money and I know plenty, especially about forms and applications!"

Still, Sarah wondered and her question remained unanswered. How were they signposted to the attempt to gain money via her personal income?

Since Mary refused to involve a solicitor, the errors she made were inevitable. Her conduct was misguided, with self-interest playing a part. She liked to be in control and her ignorance of proper procedure had made her easy prey for an unscrupulous individual.

* * *

Without a doubt, the situation must have presented the sharp-eyed young woman who interviewed the twins with no problems at all and it was easy for her to convince them of their wisdom in selecting her company's funeral services.

In preference to a boring sister, who so carefully attempted explanations they did not want to hear and could not understand, as soon as they arrived at the undertakers' rooms, Mary and Kathy were perfectly disposed to admire Eileen. They were impressed by her uniform and slender, blonde beauty. For her part, she was quick to give them her first name, engaging their trust.

Eileen made sure she seemed kind. When the two women entered her office, where antique furniture shone with polish and a graceful display of white lilies and carnations adorned the window bay, she immediately arranged for them to be served with coffee. An assistant brought their tray, making light of its weight. A tall silver pot steamed from its spout and there were gleaming teaspoons, white porcelain cups and bowls, and miniature silver jugs. The most generous quantities of cream, milk, brown *and* white sugar were supplied and crisp, foil-wrapped caramel biscuits (upon enthusiastic examination) were discovered to be *French!* The very moment Kathy mentioned she preferred sweeteners as a rule, not sugar, Eileen sent the assistant away to find a packet she just knew was in the kitchen, and the woman complied, clipping across the polished floor on high heels.

Eileen personally supervised filling the coffee cups, before declaring she would not sit *so far away* whereupon she moved her chair to a place in front of her vast, polished desk. There, she faced the twins, leaning forward confidentially, displaying a disarming combination of the powerful ice-queen image and an intense desire to be gracious.

She listened, with nods of encouragement, to Mary's issues regarding payment and learned of the existence of a sister who had been excluded from plans so far but who was targeted for paying their bill. Kathy remained silent while Mary explained that their younger sister was a nervous type of person, and they thought it best if she was simply offered a way forward.

"A fait accompli?" Eileen asked. Baffled, the women stared at her for a moment but, hastening to offer reassurances, Eileen explained she had already thought about their potential issues and difficulties! She had worked on the account, bringing costs down *especially* for just such a situation! She would do everything she could, to accommodate them. Following this speech, there was a general air of relief. Mary and Kathy drank their coffee and relaxed.

(In fact, as Sarah was to discover, Eileen made the sum fractionally under three-and-a-half thousand pounds with the trick employed in supermarkets. The full amount, apparently revised, was less than it might have been but not much! It looked better in writing.)

How tempting it was, to believe costs could be assigned to Sarah! The twins felt their worries ease; they masked grief with hilarity and allowed themselves to be guided by the immaculate Eileen. This was much easier than wasting time in research! Now, they would ignore the various alternative routes to achieving a respectful and fitting funeral service for Jeff.

Eileen knew she had a guaranteed job. She recommended a government form and said they would be allowed to delegate their responsibility. Privately, she could guess that (even after they found they may not use the form) these churchgoing ladies would find a way to keep up appearances and settle the debt. From circumstance and chatter, she could no doubt deduce that if Sarah fought, the sisters would never believe her.

It was a confidence trick therefore, and it was really quite clever.

PLEASE APPLY

On the first page of the document recommended by Eileen there appeared a question:

Are you the person who arranged the funeral? (Answer yes or no).

There followed a statement:

If you are not, you cannot use this form.

The first page? The twins must never have read it! An unwelcome thought occurred to Sarah and the more she pondered over it, the more likely it seemed. Perhaps they *were* aware of the facts and believed they could persuade her to lie? They must have assured one another of a real chance of fooling officialdom and once they were convinced of it, they probably expected Sarah to go ahead without question. Hence, the emphasis on her need to understand that some documents were already signed and she was obliged to co-operate. She wondered again, how they imagined she would cope with all the other questions and demands which emphatically ruled out her application.

Further pages required all Jeff's financial details and those of each family member. Both the sisters who arranged the funeral and signed papers were in employment, so the funding body would rule out a grant and might even launch an investigation into an unlawful application. It was clear that a claimant would need to be Jeff's live-in carer or partner, already in receipt of benefits and without anyone at all to turn to for financial assistance.

Eileen had taken note of the sisters' speculation about Sarah's finances and shamelessly turned it to her own advantage. Dismissing the possibility that there could be repercussions for herself (since she had effectively impressed the twins with her skills and sensibilities) straight-faced she proposed arrangements for government funding, all the while concealing her knowledge of truly complex criteria. Considering her position in a company of funeral directors, she could not have been unaware that she was advising clients who could never access such funding.

Extortion (The Theory)

Extortion is the attempt to gain money or property from an individual by forceful persuasion and it is a criminal activity, regardless of its ultimate success or failure.

Unlawful methods can be verbal, via text or email, or written and mailed in hard copy. The instigator of the process will do their best to present a convincing persona. They will declare a right to make demands. However, the declaration is false; no right exists and there is no moral or actual justification for access to the target individual with extortion in mind, or for the attempted persuasion of that individual to adopt the proposed course of action.

Attempted extortion involves threats. Efforts to convince the victim that compliance is essential may be disbelieved and argued, at first. In the event that deliberately forceful behaviour ensues, it constitutes intimidation (even without a violent or overtly aggressive act). The subject is entitled to report the matter to police.

Extortion (The Process)

Sarah was selected to settle her sisters' debt after Mary assumed superiority and acted on an idea. Kathy followed her twin's lead without questioning its validity. Eileen welcomed them both, listened to their plan and offered a route to securing monies. It was not lawful but it led the pair to believe they could extort money from their younger sister.

Eileen cloaked her unlawful advice in disingenuous kindness, assumption of high class and apparent professionalism, a collection of affectations which fooled Mary and Kathy completely.

* * *

"Mary! I signed off! I don't even *have* benefits!"

"Re-register then," her sister persisted. "Or sign in again, or whatever it is you claimants have to do. Anyway, you haven't got a husband or a partner now, and you are on a low income. So, you can get benefits!"

Sarah felt as if it was getting hard to breathe. "None of my personal circumstances now mean I can apply for funeral costs on a form meant for *benefits claimants* ... " She hesitated. There were tears in her eyes and she did not want to speak on a sob. She tried to gather her thoughts and began again. "Anyway ..."

She was going to point out that she had not been actively involved in caring for Jeff, but Mary interrupted her. Stubbornly, she reaffirmed her beliefs with a damaging combination of guesswork and blame. "I bet you do qualify! Don't be selfish, Sarah! Fill in the parts that make it work! It's your duty to sort it out, for all of us!"

* * *

The funeral director had seized an opportunity but Sarah couldn't help wondering if there was a more significant person in the background. Surely, the original idea of making Sarah access funds came from someone else? Did they arrive at their appointment with Eileen having already been convinced that they could raise the subject? Mary was determined that Sarah would accompany them to the meeting and dismayed when she refused. What was the plan? To what extent had it taken shape, by that time?

Sarah could not know the exact reason why she became her sisters' target because they would not talk to her fairly, but it was hard to believe that Mary had invented the plan alone. Kathy was merely a copier. She saw that her presence at the funeral directors' offices (had she attended) might have been the start of some very confrontational, coercive behaviour from the twins and it would have happened in that setting.

Once the extent of their scheme was revealed, she could only suspect that chatter in the charity centre was to blame. The twins didn't bother to conceal the fact that Sarah's situation had been discussed, so it seemed that some uninformed individual felt free to offer Mary an opinion.

With the use of persuasion and emotional blackmail, attempts to make Sarah believe that she was legally obliged to fall into line with a contrived claim were certainly based upon speculation about her private circumstances. It was founded on a set of erroneous beliefs.

Entitlements

(i)   Extra income from the government.

(ii) A grant for a funeral (regardless of personal circumstances / circumstances hitherto relating to Jeff / whether or not other members of Jeff's family could afford to pay the bill).

Duties

(i)   To secure money to pay Mary's bill, which was set up without prior arrangement because speculative conversations led to a belief that her sister's financial circumstances seemed to suit the cause.

(ii) To write such comments and reports as seemed expedient into a legal document, even if this meant lying to suit the cause.

(iii) To perceive herself essentially duty bound to comply because she was Jeff's sister.

(iv) To comply regardless of any discussion *even if* her financial circumstances did not suit their cause, because she was a family member and therefore bound to adopt the same course of action as her sisters.

* * *

It was a thoroughly corrupt idea. With shameless encouragement from the calculating Eileen, the twins' determination to extort money was forceful. They wanted their sister to arrange a new dependency on government aid, specifically for the purpose of settling a debt she had not agreed. They were unable to understand that such a retrospective effort would look obvious, even criminal.

When Sarah pointed out the flaws in their plan, she tried to explain that her duties did not exist as perceived by the twins. She had no existing entitlements and could not arrange new ones! Then, the twins' efforts went beyond reasonable persuasion. With derisive comments and attempts to ridicule her views and belittle her experience, they refused to allow for the fact that she had knowledge and rights. They tried to frighten her into compliance.

Mary warned that Sarah risked wrongdoing and ensuing personal embarrassment; furthermore, the whole family would be disappointed if she failed to comply. Stepping up the emotional pressure, together the twins became threatening when they said they knew she would create legal problems, since official documents had been signed on her behalf.

Sarah was sent written details of the specific sum of the demand, emphatic declarations of urgency and false assurances that application to her was a result of expert advice, responsibly accessed.

A Real Crime

Eileen was determined to secure the commission and her sights were set firmly on promoting her company. First and foremost, she was not the compassionate friend she pretended to be but a hard-bitten business woman. She had many ploys and the twins were taken in. They were victims, convinced by a façade of professionalism and childishly hopeful that, in presenting their sister with a form they did not understand, they would resolve their dilemma. Perhaps they believed that their consultation with the woman meant they really had secured legal advice.

Sarah couldn't know all the details of that interview but she looked up the firm of funeral directors on the internet, saw pictures of Eileen and knew the twins must have been impressed by her black costume, which even included, on occasion, a hat extravagantly adorned with a glossy ebony feather! (An aspect of the sisters' contempt for Sarah was her choice of clothing. She was generally perfectly content to wear a flower-print skirt and a cardigan or sweater which had seen better days, unless she was dressed for work or a special occasion. Unlike the twins, she had no slavish love of fashion or fondness for stuffing herself into tight-fitting outfits.)

Although Sarah knew she could not be pushed to change, especially in haste and without talks, she felt upset. However, after a few days had passed, her thoughts were less frantic. She continued to be uneasy about the twins' expectations but she began to wonder if they could be innocent of deliberate wrongdoing, since they were grief-stricken. At this vulnerable time, a highly manipulative woman had surely chosen to mislead them instead of pointing out their mistake. The lack of wisdom, mused Sarah, is not a crime.

This train of thought did not excuse the twins' refusal to discuss things properly, or their initial concealment of the intention to force her to pay! Surely, they should have visited their sister to go over the form together, instead of posting it and hoping for a good result? Sarah's kind-hearted attempt to comprehend the world of Mary and Kathy failed when she reviewed their angry responses to her efforts to communicate! Her conclusion had to be that they cared little or nothing for her peace of mind but she decided to end her sense of intimidation.

Bullies are only successful if the victim is afraid!

She focused on making her advice really clear. She would turn the other cheek! They had drawn her into their plans; surely, they could not throw her out again, just because their selected route to gaining funds must change?

The twins may have developed a belief that Sarah had scant understanding of legal processes, since her husband was able to escape with her money. They had never asked her how it happened. Nevertheless, she reasoned, they knew she had been studying and for any logical person her knowledge of procedure and experience in bereavement services should have counted. She was well respected by many other people. Sarah decided she could try to explain something of her history, her rights and her sensible way of thinking.

She began by brainstorming and wrote down a collection of thoughts, which she scribbled in a pocket notebook when important details occurred to her. At last, she progressed to drafting an email in which she detailed reasons why the form was not safe. There was a risk of perceived fraud and one cannot make something unlawful fit circumstances. She stayed up late into the night to perfect this and, when it was complete, she attached a personal message, trying to achieve the perfect balance between seeming business-like and friendly. She must make her points clear but it was a difficult task and she was acutely aware that all her previous messages had been ignored.

For some minutes, sitting in front of her computer, thinking hard, Sarah tried to make herself face the possibility that she, too was being disingenuous! Mary had written a letter which was intended to look both business-like and friendly. She had included firm expressions of her belief in Sarah's duties, her certainty of the best way forward and instructions too. She had added pictures and kisses, to try to make her message more acceptable and convince Sarah of her affection. The effort was transparent and the pictures devalued it. It was a letter written with self-interest in mind, but what was the difference between herself and her sister? Realism? Sarah checked the term in a dictionary and her understanding matched the definition. *When thoughts and actions are based on facts and on what may be possible.*

She rubbed her eyes, trying to confront a situation that was partly informed by guesswork. Mary would never talk to her, face-to-face, in a completely frank way!

Deciding that confronting reality must be essential for all three sisters, Sarah came to the conclusion that honesty was the main element she sought but it was the main difference between herself the twins. Believing she had to try her best, Sarah wrote a few thoughtful lines to add to her email and she put them at the start.

Dear Anne and Mary, this is another email and I'm sorry about that but please read it! You could take it to a solicitor if you want to. I'm trying to explain something that I think is so important ...!

The tone of Sarah's email was not patronising but she made efforts to avoid complicated detail as far as possible. She made no complaint about being left out, knowing that protestations of unfair treatment risked accusations of childishness. She offered no new invitation to share coffee and a talk because she knew the sisters wouldn't want to spend their time with her; however, she tried not to look so impartial that she could seem deliberately unfriendly.

The difficulties were genuinely similar to those of their childhood, when poor Sarah could not argue against the bullying for fear of being taunted even more; nor was it wise to lash out, since her mother would then join in with reproach. It was impossible to make herself pleasant towards the twins because they were disinterested in making friends with her. They rejected and ridiculed her, no matter what she did.

With all these obstacles to overcome, still Sarah determined to try to change the course of events. She drew on her studies in conflict resolution, looking to acknowledge the problems so far but find an agreement they could all tolerate. She offered to take over and manage dealings with the undertaker, explaining that the sisters could generously create an opportunity for Eileen to admit an error of judgement. (Sarah had guessed that Eileen's behaviour was deliberate but a disingenuous approach would be in the best interests of all concerned.) All three sisters, working together, could apply for a reduction in costs on the basis that it should be a goodwill gesture.

After labouring over this important missive for a whole evening, Sarah had constructed her very best effort. She hoped it conveyed a fairly friendly approach. She left out legal jargon, ignored the recent history and how upsetting it had been, set aside the issue of interference in her private affairs and did not attempt to seem particularly effusive. She indulged in just a little reasonable argument, pointing out her own sadness since Jeff's passing. She shared the sisters' grief. There was no reason to think she wasn't trying hard to make everything right and fair.

On the firm's website, there were extravagant claims of expertise. Although she invented a resolution with a light touch, in fact Sarah could hardly wait to call the undertakers out! She convinced herself her plan was viable.

It was all in vain. On their return from holiday, the twins treated Sarah's emails with derision! How could *she* know better than an undertaker? "Everyone" was annoyed with her! They expressed their astonishment, to think she would create such a dreadful, embarrassing argument at a time like this.

In fact, Mary and Kathy had moved on, revised their plan for acquiring money and were not open to a review of events. They dismissed the evidence of their sister's knowledge and said that, if she had not been awkward about attending an important meeting, she would understand what she should do. It was depressingly obvious that they were going to bear a grudge. They called her behaviour "bizarre" but in protecting Eileen, foolishly they protected their debt.

Perhaps they needed to defend their choices for the sake of their self-esteem? It might have been easier for them to admire a powerful stranger in preference to allowing their sister to highlight mistakes, which could lead to an uncomfortable requirement for apologies.

For Sarah, disappointed and insulted all over again, the whirling thoughts were back.

CHALLENGES

As soon as Sarah questioned the activities of the undertaker, Mary began to treat her like an enemy. She behaved as if her sister was a risk to all concerned, swiftly alerting Eileen and her associates. Nevertheless, Sarah wrote to Eileen and carefully highlighted facts. The twins had thought it appropriate to use a complicated form which would run them into trouble. It seemed their expectations might have begun in conversation with charitable acquaintances, but further conviction resulted from their discussions with Eileen herself. This had led to their deliberate attempt to involve Sarah, which was inevitable once they had been signposted to accessing government funding. They were sure their sister must share the process and, with confused memories of a time long gone, they even imagined she could take responsibility for its outcome.

The firm was powerful and it was sheltered by its status and professed ethos of compassion, as well as an artistically presented website and a smart front of uniforms and gleaming cars. The team soon fought brutally to protect their reputation. Eileen sent an email in return and her tone was caustic. She insisted she had not offered any single, specific form! Instead, she said, a set of choices were presented in the course of normal procedure. She wrote this, even though the point of recommendation was emphasised in Mary's letter. The woman was duplicitous.

Mary received telephone calls and the first came from a senior director's personal secretary. The woman was well-spoken and brisk in her manner. She asked Mary's permission for the director to call by appointment, to discuss "the situation which has arisen". Flattered, Mary graciously gave her consent and the call came.

The director introduced himself. He was the firm's senior partner and he hoped Mary would call him by his first name, which was Adam. He affected grave and solicitous concern. He said he had given the matter careful consideration and his professional opinion (if he might offer it) was that her sister, in her grief, had become confused. He was used to seeing this effect. He firmly believed that Mary was doing the right thing by her sisters and (regrettably) he doubted Sarah understood the extent of her duties to her family.

Veiled in the appearance of deepest respect for Mary's autonomy, the call was extremely cunning and highly manipulative. The director made sure to address Mary's grandiosity. Saying he was well-used to the effects of confused thinking, he elevated his bearing on the matter and placed Sarah in a vulnerable position.

The director was then able to tap into and use Mary's preferred attitude towards her sister: Sarah was being deliberately annoying and she was profoundly in the wrong. His engaging comments, designed to deflect attention away from Eileen's behaviour, made a victim of Mary but she was unable to recognise it! Instead, she gladly acquiesced. She certainly had been encouraged to think she could use and delegate the form but now, with praise for her ability to discern, she was essentially being required to overlook this important fact, to believe its selection was her own, wise decision. After the director's call, she turned her attention to Sarah, contacted her and expressed absolute rage. What did Sarah think she was doing, writing to the woman who had helped and supported the twins so kindly? How did Sarah have the nerve to interfere in something that wasn't her business?

"You made it my business!" Sarah pointed out.

"You weren't even there!" Mary screamed.

Sarah took a breath. She ignored Mary's comment in terms of the depth of meaning behind it. (No, she was not there but she had offered a discussion ahead of formal arrangements. The twins should not have set up such a meeting in her absence.) Instead, she maintained her point. Her sister's accusations were illogical. "You involved me, didn't you? When you delegated a form and required me to deal with it … and pay …?"

The response was breath-taking. "You only needed to sign the form!" Clearly, a suspicion had been correct. Mary had never opened and read the document before she sent it to her sister!

By this time, Sarah could tell that Eileen had the complicity of her business partners and was unscrupulous. She was easily capable of maintaining two different assertions. The first was, the twins were free to make their plans as they saw fit. This was a lie created in order to argue against Sarah's intelligent awareness. However, for Eileen's clients, the story (and second untruth) was that the form was suitable. She flattered Mary, encouraging her delusions. She let the twins believe that, in the most intelligent of approaches, she deemed it an unfortunate eventuality when Sarah refused to address her duties.

Sarah was supplied, via email, with Mary's interpretation of the director's telephone conversation but she could not fight the convolutions of his arguments or the twins' failure to grasp the truth while her every word was being cast aside. They would certainly dismiss the letter she was sent, if she had the temerity to produce it in an effort to show Eileen's behaviour differed according to circumstances. They were not able or willing to identify Eileen's duplicity for themselves and they had no interest in an examination of the proof. Sarah could not prove her point therefore, and neither twin was thoughtful enough to seek legal advice.

The director's judicious inclusion of a spot of amateur psychoanalysis in his conversation seemed to form a credible basis for his pomposity. He fed into Mary's wish to assume superior knowledge and to dismiss Sarah as nonsensical: a perception the twins always maintained in the past, fostered, unfortunately, by Lena. Mary gladly accepted his affected knowledge and description of the psychology of mourning. She liked his explanation of her sister's perceived contrariness and could not guess why it was offered; nor could she wait to accuse Sarah of being unable to see things clearly as a result of her "confusion" and inability to understand that the twins were in the right.

"You always think there's a conspiracy!" Mary told her sister. "You don't see things clearly! You could at least have *tried* to help us!" Her words were uniquely unkind, for indeed Sarah would have helped and she envisaged much to be done, even though she couldn't go along with a dishonest plan. On the subject of "a conspiracy" she was hardly blinkered! Certainly, there had been one.

In a psychological effect known as projection, Mary's thoughts immediately turned around Sarah's awareness that the twins had essentially conducted quite a plot. Now Mary tried to deflect blame and accuse Sarah herself of failures and deception!

On some level, Mary must have realised she had been caught out but she would not allow this to surface into conscious thought or deliberation and her narcissism kept her from addressing the possibility she could be in the wrong.

For Sarah, there was only one way forward and it was to ensure compliance with the law. She made an appeal for arbitration to an official organisation, detailing the damage caused to herself and confirming there was misguidance by the undertakers' company, which potentially posed risks to other customers if this was common practice.

Her application was quickly rejected. She could tell it was barely addressed in fact, suspected swift telephone calls had been made to the directors' offices and knew a defensive response was aimed at putting her off. If she highlighted and proved there had been duplicity, she would cause real trouble if she took the case to court. She was keen to do so but with the funeral arrangements swept away from her, it proved impossible to pursue the issue alone. No-one was willing to back her up. Kathy and Mary were the ones who had met with Eileen in that grand office, were so impressed they were unable to be discerning and they would never question the information they were handed that day, or compare it with their sister's knowledge. If only Mary could grasp the nature of Eileen's confidence trick or was open to discussion about the way the directors had persuaded her of their integrity, Sarah could have made a case! It was no use, since neither twin could fully comprehend what had happened to them. To them, Eileen had dutifully recommended Sarah's involvement in the debt, not only as a safe plan which anyone might adopt but as something which (she encouraged them to imagine) began with their own, clever idea.

Even to suggest the form *might* be an option was a profoundly irresponsible thing to do but Eileen's advice (like her self-presentation) was perfect in their eyes. Their sister's refusal, coupled with her warning that the ultimate result could be court proceedings, met with their contempt. They envied Sarah for her fair prettiness and saw her as someone to resent. They recognised Eileen's fair beauty too, but thought she presented no challenge. In fact, they could not understand that their unquestioning admiration of Eileen was far more dangerous than a more natural respect for their sister!

So, if there was a failure to understand the situation, it was Mary's problem, especially after she acquired a huge debt but since she admired her deceiver Eileen, then Sarah, it must be, who was acting strangely. Mary continued to believe Sarah should have allowed herself to be collected and taken to the meeting with the funeral director. She was certain that if all three sisters had been present, Sarah's duty to obtain funding might somehow have been impressed upon on her, forms would bear her signature and she would have been obliged to fall into line!

Kathy was doubly a victim. Copying Mary, taking sides, she was affected, not only by corrupt treatment from the funeral firm but also by her twin sister's foolish narcissism. With a lofty disregard for the reality of the situation, Mary would not entertain the possibility that she had made a mistake. She dismissed the significance of her younger sister's true independence and deluded herself into thinking a low income led to an entitlement to government help, regardless of the system.

It was *embarrassing*, Mary insisted, that Sarah, having been absent, had subsequently interested and involved herself in arrangements they had already made with Eileen. Arrangements, said Mary, *which were not her business!*

As one of a trio of sisters to Jeff, Sarah had certain moral rights and the twins had shown awful disregard for her genuine role in the family. They ignored the importance of an early meeting between them all, before taking the step of deciding how to manage and pay for the funeral. Sarah considered such plans certainly might have been none of her business, in a way, had they not resulted in an outcome it was proposed she should finance! In the past she had become fairly resigned to the habitual behaviour of the twins. Perhaps, if they had found a valid route to creating a respectful funeral, avoiding their extortion attempt, she could have let her part go? She tried to help nonetheless, then stood back only after her warnings were dismissed and all her efforts to share duties were rejected.

Kathy sent a comment to the effect that Sarah should have respected the process. She didn't know how her sister could bear to be so *selfish*. Then, both women continued to express fury in emails. Their intentions to be hurtful were so obvious, Sarah began to delete new messages without reading them.

* * *

Projection

In an exercise that is usually unconscious, an individual who is harbouring an unkind attitude towards another may make accusations, trying to pinpoint the same feeling *in that person*. This is simple to explain, in a way. It's an attempt to shift the blame for an uncomfortable relationship, making it the burden and responsibility of the other person.

In the case, for instance, of the first individual being contemptuous of the sensitivities of the second, they will label that person "rude". Someone who feels envious might tell another that he or she is "always jealous"! The behaviour is particularly frustrating for the victim, who is often met with ridicule if they seek to examine and discuss the nature of such argument.

The Sisters

When Mary accused her younger sister of having "a distorted mind", in fact she, herself, had an exceptionally grand estimation of her own importance. Her belief in the extent of her abilities was not based on facts; she did not possess the training needed to comprehend processes she was flinging herself into and she could have been shown to be delusional, if only she had listened to reason.

Kathy insisted Sarah was competitive but it was she who failed to look at their situation impartially. She took Mary's side, buying into the concept of a battle of sorts. Trying blindly to add weight to the argument against Sarah's viewpoint, she was always looking to further the case for using of their form. In an inappropriate spirit of competition, essentially uninformed, she entered into efforts to create a situation over which her younger sister had no control.

Sarah knew only too well, if she had protested more strongly with emphasis on her right to play her part, she would have been reminded the twins thought Mary knew best and shouldn't be challenged. In any display of emotion, she would have been ridiculed all the more harshly. While the twins expressed their anger and perceived distress freely at all times, if Sarah did the same, she would have been accused of weakness.

THE FUNERAL

The twins had made no secret of their belief that their sister let them down. It was painful to be aware of this. Sarah would really have to keep her chin up at the funeral! Would there be questioning, even unfriendly glances from other mourners? The date approached and she didn't relish the prospect of facing her sisters but she resolved not to let them force her away. Calls from her daughter were comforting. Celeste had decided to spend a year living and working abroad but she was in constant contact with her mother and knew the date of the sad occasion ahead.

Sarah insisted she should continue with her plans. In study and travel, Celeste enjoyed experiences denied to Sarah herself during her youth and she felt proud, and knew her encouragement and support were enabling her daughter to pursue her ambitions.

The day arrived at last. Sarah had made up her mind not to feel daunted and she didn't dread it. The opportunity to pay her respects to her brother along with many others who were there to do the same, would be of some comfort. Remembering how he used to praise her, she decided to make herself look very smart. Her black suit, with a slim, straight skirt, was sober attire but she wore a cream-coloured blouse under the jacket with a small lace collar showing. She pinned her hair into a smooth, blonde swirl before adding a sparkling ornament.

"You've still got beautiful eyes!" Jeff's words came into Sarah's mind. She had to find a tissue for tears but when she was ready to face her mirror again, she put on some make-up. She brushed a soft rose blusher along her cheekbones, smudged a little smoky shadow on her lids and swept grey mascara along her lashes. The touches of subtle colour gave her eyes blue depths. With a spray of floral perfume, her preparations were complete.

"I am a competent woman!" Sarah reminded her reflection in the mirror. Her responses to the sisters could lead to times when she felt like nothing more than a child. With sorrow lending an ethereal quality to her skin and eyes, at forty-six she looked years younger but she was not about to let herself be fearful now.

Footsteps crunched over a broad gravel path and people made their way beneath tall, dark fir trees to enter the church. Many of the mourners were dressed casually, even colourfully. Comments were enlightening when others mentioned instructions to wear bright clothes. Sadly, Sarah remembered the long night when she stayed by Jeff's side and fought for his right to be free of pain as he slipped away, taking with him those plans and ideas for a book. She was not abashed to be dressed in the traditional black and thought everyday styles were not a fitting tribute when her beloved brother had lost so many years of life ahead. When someone dies, Sarah thought, it's no use pretending their funeral is a party.

An old man sat in a wheelchair that was being guided carefully through the modest gathering by a uniformed young woman. Covered with a thick blanket over his knees and looking frail, this was the relative who had agreed to settle the costs of the funeral. He glanced at Sarah, nodded briefly then looked away. He was Eddie's distant cousin but (regardless of their actual relation to him) everyone in the family always referred to him, affectionately, as "Uncle Bill".

When Sarah was very young, Bill often visited her grandmother and would speak to the child kindly as she played there, setting out her dolls on a rug by the fire or rolling pencils for the elderly cat to chase. He would delve into the pockets of his loose, tweed jacket for toffees or peppermints. One afternoon, he sat down with a tray and a pack of cards, called the little girl to stand at his knee and patiently explained how to play a card game.

As prayers were said and familiar hymns sung, it was difficult for Sarah to control troubled thoughts, especially when a realisation suddenly hit her with force. If Mary told Uncle Bill that Sarah blocked their entitlement to funds by a petty refusal to join an essential meeting, he certainly would think badly of her. She suspected false information had been given to this kind man since, for sure, he would normally have greeted her pleasantly and shown an interest in her wellbeing.

"I'm guessing," she scolded herself crossly, feeling saddened. She was powerless to address that false impression. The initiation of a discussion and potential argument would not have been appropriate in this setting and if she contemplated raising the matter at a later date, she knew it was probable, in an unfair twist, that *she* could appear to be the person who told lies!

Sarah stood upright, holding the hymn sheet, not singing. Her hands and feet felt cold and she rearranged a scarf at her neck and tucked her chin more deeply inside it.

A new thought tormented her. If the sisters had not attempted their onslaught on her own finances, she might have seen their uncle simply as a benefactor. Thanks to his generosity, the sad occasion was conducted with due ceremony. Would Sarah have felt free to accept the old gentleman's gift, if she had not been so upset? Would she have stood alongside her sisters, in agreement?

The answer had to be "no", since Bill was an unwitting victim of Mary's determined effort to control the situation. He could have kept his money for his own grandchildren if Sarah had been respected and if she had been free to make some of the arrangements which, in truth, she had the expertise to manage.

She glanced around at the congregation and could see Bill, who looked smart with his thick iron-grey hair neatly brushed and a dark jacket above the warm rug that covered his knees. It would not be appropriate to offer him her personal thanks when friends and relatives gathered for refreshments, later. She couldn't, because she wasn't in accord with the twins. Now, her train of thought had brought her back in a circle to the fact that she had been side-lined, so firmly that it felt impossible to greet her uncle warmly, talk freely, or address the truth of the matter with him. Where would the conversation go next? She knew he was a victim, the subject of grave financial fraud. Sarah could hardly pretend to agree that he was required to settle Mary's debt; she could not make any disingenuous comment, not even to express her respect. She could not risk plunging into a conversation about recent events.

Sarah would always remember that, with her support, the matter could have been righted without one individual shouldering the full responsibility to pay. The whole business was a real family tragedy and it made their great loss even sadder.

Perhaps, thought Sarah, a letter might be written and sent privately to Bill? Could she express her gratitude carefully, in writing, leaving out the most painful aspects of the truth, or would those all crowd in, as she wrote such a letter? Was there, in fact, any way to show how the disagreements with the sisters had unfolded? Even as the thought occurred to her, she knew she would feel sly and wrong to attempt to find a route to justify herself in that way, and after all, she would be guessing in terms of the extent of Bill's understanding of events so far. He was a very old man who might find the situation confusing. Doubtless, he would want to show the letter to the twins. A similar problem to the history of communications with the funeral directors could easily follow. To Sarah's troubled mind, there seemed no resolution to the dilemma.

She found her voice to join in with hymn singing and listened to the eulogies, letting the service pass with its inevitable dreamlike quality. It was, in many ways, a fair expression of loving memories of Jeff. The mourners left the crematorium eventually, making their way to rooms in a local pub where walls were painted white and criss-crossed with black beams, long tables held a generous buffet and there was blissful warmth. The atmosphere felt calming and better. Relieved, Sarah unwound her scarf from her neck and shed her outer coat.

She filled her plate with salad from the serving dishes, added cheese and a buttered roll, then collected a glass of orange juice from the bar and seated herself near a good-natured person whom she recognised. When she confessed to being uncertain about how they knew one another, the woman explained.

"I used to serve you and the other children in the shop! I remember you and Jeff, with your big eyes and fair fringes!" She was one of many acquaintances who had attended the funeral with a genuine wish to support the family. "I'm Michelle," she went on. She gave Sarah a careful glance. "You should get a glass of wine, dear!"

Michelle wore her hair very short and she was dressed in a smart outfit with a corsage made of black and purple flowers pinned to her lapel. It was comforting to chat with her, but Sarah's response to this remark was a smile and shake of the head. "I'm driving," she said. "I might get one later, after I get home!"

When she collected her coat from a row of hooks in a dark hallway, her heart was heavy but the sisters were disinterested, turning their backs, refilling their glasses. They were both tightly zipped and buttoned into new dresses and the idea of wearing bright colours must have been theirs. A piece of modern music was being played but Sarah didn't know if it was something Jeff had enjoyed. For her part, she could think of nothing worth saying to the twins, there with warm-hearted companions, most of whom knew only that the three women were grieving for their brother.

She shrugged herself into her coat, retied her scarf and turned up her collar. Quietly, she unlatched the heavy door and pushed it with her palm. It swung open with a faint creak, a breath of cool air blew against her face and she left.

THE FLAT

Despite his artistic brilliance, throughout his lifetime Jeff suffered from poor self-esteem. It was the inevitable result of the relative disinterest of his mother combined with harsh criticism from his father, which harmed the child's developing perception of himself and his worth. In this way, a sense of being unworthy became a personality trait.

As an adult, his beautiful paintings were admired by all those who were fortunate enough to have sight of them, but most of his canvasses were eventually handed over to friends or even casual acquaintances, as gifts. Jeff was no businessman, nor did he care much for money and he had no interest in saving his income in order to accumulate wealth or protect himself. He casually spent nearly all the money he earned from bartending, seasonal farm work and occasionally, building.

A likeable person, he had integrity and people responded to him with warmth. He was seldom turned away from new employment but his money disappeared fast. His natural charm and enjoyment of living in the moment without worrying about the future won him many genuine friends. Often, he treated his companions to an expensive restaurant meal or even a holiday. In a reciprocal gesture, a close friend offered him accommodation, rent free. During the few months Jeff spent in England after his travels and before his illness began to affect him, he stayed in a spacious flat in London.

* * *

Sarah kept trying to bring order into the chaos of hurt feelings and angry accusations. The thought of Jeff's belongings, lying untouched, was very sad. She suggested all three sisters might visit the flat together after Jeff died, in order to take care of the possessions he left behind. Perhaps they could talk while they got on with the tasks?

Mary and Kathy reacted with annoyance. They would do it all, they insisted. She had never been there and didn't need to go! It was an accusation of sorts, intended to be insulting. In their shared view, the fact Sarah hadn't visited Jeff in his home meant she was not to join in with clearing it, now. They had been there together, they said, after his diagnosis, so they knew far more than their sister about his circumstances and his lifestyle. Sarah had no way of knowing whether or not this was true, although Jeff had not mentioned the twins when she saw him in the hospice. There seemed to be no words to express how childish it was, to exclude her from the essential task.

Kathy remarked that she wondered what Sarah thought she would find. It was an unpleasant hint that Sarah appeared to be hoping for something of value that she might take for herself. Staggeringly spiteful and intentional, the comment was so unexpected, it reminded Sarah that she never knew what insult might next be slung her way. Of course, she could have turned it around! What did Kathy and Mary expect to find? Did they think they could spot something valuable and protect it from Sarah? Instead, tired of cruel insults, she stood back.

Ironically (or perhaps it was inevitable), at a later date she was to learn the pair returned to London and ransacked the flat. They found Jeff's new computer and printer, cameras, a fistful of cash in a bedside drawer as well as cheques and various personal documents including a passport. They took everything and did not list it, and the subsequent revelation came directly from Kathy, who undoubtedly took a certain satisfaction in the implicit challenge to any interest Sarah might dare to reveal in the whereabouts of the sisters' loot. With no illusions left for them to shatter, she resolved to ignore this extra slight.

* * *

It had been a hopeless attempt to discuss the flat and Sarah knew that; yet she felt guilty because she wanted to protect and treasure her brother's possessions. After Kathy saw fit to send an email for the express purpose of delivering the information that she and Mary had emptied Jeff's former home, Sarah had a renewed physical response to her distress, with a hot face and trembling. She successfully withheld comment but, in truth, she felt unsure about how much annoyance to reveal. No doubt, in many ways the sisters deserved to be held to account for their appalling behaviour. It seemed impossible to shake off remembered childhood bullying when, if she retaliated, it was she who ran into parental disapproval. With those thoughts and memories, Sarah suffered again.

At bedtime, she made malted milk, which was the drink her grandmother gave her when she was small. She piled up pillows and lay against them, feeling cosy with a silky quilt covering her knees and a warm orange-coloured blanket wrapped around her shoulders. The purring cat joined her, settled and curled up tightly on her chest.

Stroking her pet's black fur, Sarah experimented with a perception. Her sisters asked her to help. Could she have been more amenable? Friendlier? Easier to talk to?

For all the reasons she gave them, it would have been impossible. She really ought to have been consulted about the best course of action before a funeral service was booked and even if she elected to overlook inappropriate interest in her money, everyone involved would have broken the law if that form was used. Their assumptions about entitlement were wrong. Sarah dismissed this brief, factual review and moved on to consider the emotional responses of each of her sisters and herself.

If she had simply set aside her moral judgment, firmly declined the form and then stood back completely, was it possible that petty insults would have been prevented? Perhaps that *was* so, for the women certainly saw her as someone to fight! They detested her resistance but they also blindly rejected her explanations. However, they would surely have been infuriated in exactly the same way, when their plan was thwarted! With Mary's affectations of superior knowledge, they had invented a course of action which (given their history of manipulating Sarah) they cherished, for a time.

It was too late to alter all that had happened but Sarah's tired brain seemed to be trying to force her to persist with her review. Could she have stopped every one of her comments, when the twins returned from their holiday with a new plan? Should she have set aside the explanations she'd prepared and let them get on with asking Uncle Bill for money? Should she have realised they would never let her share a trip to the flat?

Looking back, knowing she was the subject of discussion and a target for money, Sarah knew she had needed to go through the experience in her own way. Assumptions based on misinformation, slyly shared with others, were never going to be acceptable; she had wanted to try to show her sisters how wrong their plans were. In her mind, the possibility of success had been real on occasion, causing her to pursue a train of thought, trying to be generous, wanting to play her part. She was a very different thinker from Kathy and Mary. There was nothing to be done about her hurt feelings but at last she was beginning to understand that, in future, there would be no need to address furious accusations.

Sarah concluded that her self-imposed guilty torment should end, especially as no one else was ever likely to care! She had been sunk in her reflections for over an hour; sleepiness was beginning to feel overwhelming. She was still clutching her empty mug. With a sigh, she placed it on the table at the bedside, buried herself comfortably in her nest of bedclothes and closed her eyes.

After sleeping deeply at first, in the early hours of the morning Sarah drifted into a lighter doze. Her mind became active, her thoughts troubled; she fidgeted. She became dimly aware that her tumbling bedclothes were uncomfortable, yet she remained too sleepy to waken fully.

She found herself picturing a scenario in which she went along with Mary's instructions to attend the meeting with the funeral director. In this imaginary setting, she sat before three women while they assured her that they knew her financial circumstances, so it was essential to sign their form. She became obsessional, trying to make herself think of something to say that was so clever, it would put an end to their efforts for good. In the way of people who have suffered from untruthful accusations, again she struggled with shocked feelings, contemplating a possibility that she, herself, was profoundly in the wrong.

Dreaming still, yet with a sense of being back in her bed and a powerful sense of reality, Sarah thought she saw her father sitting beside her! He seemed to hand over an object. "Here," he said. "Daughter, take it all with *a pinch of salt!*"

Sarah stretched out an arm. She was aware of cool air against her skin and found herself wide awake, feeling confused. Yes, she *had* reached out! Her hand was raised, palm uppermost, ready to receive the salt cellar she thought was there. She rubbed her eyes and realised her vision was only an intense illusion. She was alone except for the indignant black cat, who leapt from slipping bedcovers.

In the garden, birds began to chirrup and pale light gleamed behind the thin material of closed curtains. Sarah abandoned sleep and went to the kitchen to brew tea. Clasping a steaming mug, she found herself restlessly pacing through the house, trying to imagine an end to her confusion, knowing she needed to free herself. As the morning brightened, she dressed in warm clothes, found a pair of boots and went out through the cream-painted, latched door of her cottage.

Fresh air was reviving. Sarah made her way to the narrow track that led from the tiny square of her front garden, heading towards a pathway. She traversed patches of muddy allotments, saw clusters of early snowdrops and walked on, through a thin coppice of trees. Dawn passed, birdsong abated and her mind began to find its strength.

The dream wasn't hard to understand. Long ago, her parents insisted she should not think badly of her sisters no matter what they did. Her father, if he were here, certainly would advise against a deeper analysis of the situation, or creating further upsetting scenes. Sarah thought about the words which, half-asleep, she thought were so clear.

"Take it all with a pinch of salt!"

She tried to imagine how a proper conversation might have gone, if only Eddie was here and still the man he was before poor Lena passed away. When she remembered her father, part of her sorrow was that his occasional cruelty was mixed with high intelligence. She respected him to a great extent, but her childish love and longing to honour him had been harmed. He had confused her.

"It doesn't matter what the twins do, now!" Sarah imagined he'd say. "You can let it go!"

Was that fair? Sarah's reputation may have been trashed, Uncle Bill would not share a conversation and she was still feeling hurt and angry. Were Mary and Kathy going to leave her alone, from now on? Could she live with the distress they had so carelessly caused?

It would have been kind of their parents to step in, years ago, to put a stop to the bullying, she thought stubbornly. Look where those old ways got us, then and this time, too! In fact, both Eddie and Lena were more likely to ignore the three girls, regardless of their duty to care for each one in a sympathetic way. Still, she returned to the message in the dream. Could she be more *philosophical?* Perhaps, while a victim should abandon self-reproach, it was important to let go of hatred, too? Was it wrong to believe that fault lies with anyone at all?

Some questions remained, Sarah thought. If a premise might be that a course of events could unfold without any person being culpable, when you think about how crimes are committed, and wars begin, that simply cannot be true! Sometimes, people must be held accountable for their actions. She began to wonder what precipitates disastrous behaviour.

Psychoanalysis

Over several years, Sarah trained in aspects of psychology. She was well-equipped to comprehend much human behaviour but she enjoyed extra studies. With a firm belief that knowledge could only enhance her counselling skills, she was very careful to keep a low profile in any new course; she was not there to promote herself and was always aware that a tutor could feel challenged by a mature learner who seemed to understand the syllabus well. In addition to extra short courses, she attended lectures and seminars, choosing subjects that were relevant to her interests, always keeping modestly quiet as a rule.

Sometimes, case studies were both intellectually and emotionally challenging, especially when a tutor named Nicole presented topics under the heading of *Forensic Psychology*. Care was taken to protect students from deeply disturbing reflections and the case histories were described in a factual way. For most people, this led to feeling able to study without distressing images lingering in their minds.

In private study, Sarah read that the person-centred therapist named Carl Rogers stated a fundamental perfect rationality and believed this was common to all humans. In fact, she could not go along with it, considering what terrible things humankind can do! Looking carefully at debate in a topic entitled *Nature versus Nurture*, her group learned that people who were full of fun as children, can sometimes alter and become unpleasant, potentially wicked adults. Sarah raised the question. What did the tutor think of the theory held by some counsellors, that *every* individual is capable of changing and becoming altruistic?

Nicole was a glamorous woman. She had a cloud of thick, dark hair, wore a great deal of red lipstick and heady perfume which seemed to hang in the air around her. In response to Sarah's question, she rolled her eyes expressively and began an animated explanation. The training of person-centred counsellors can be short. In just two years, a diploma may be acquired but much essential, complex psychology may be neglected. In any case (she pointed out) there are a multitude of abnormal mental illnesses about which the holder of a simple diploma may know nothing! For example, there is absolutely no point in trying to counsel and change a psychopath, especially since there are abnormalities in that individual's brain.

When they debated the importance of family dynamics, inevitably Sarah remembered her sisters were not kind as youngsters. Their destructive spirit of competition was always there, and it had been disappointing and sometimes even harmful. She voiced something of her experience, mentioning that the family were grieving the loss of a younger brother.

"My impression is of *grief and pain*," said the tutor, somewhat loftily. "That's inevitable, after a bereavement."

Sarah spotted her air of superiority. Was it possible she had risen to the teaching role she held without a working understanding of psychodynamic theories? Certainly, the three sisters were all shocked and saddened by Jeff's passing but those childhood habits couldn't be denied! In the tutor's word's there was implication that there was no imbalance. Each one of the women could be so affected by their grief, they could become angry or difficult. Sarah understood that but she thought it was a dismissive response.

Privately, she reflected that, since all three were experiencing the same circumstances, there seemed no excuse for two to revive their old behaviour in order to gang up against one, causing more pain. *What about injustice?* She did not voice the question and the lesson went on.

They read papers with descriptions of all kinds of crimes. One afternoon, a grey-haired older lady, who had sat beside Sarah throughout the early sessions, became obviously uncomfortable. She said she couldn't bear to think about the victims. She gathered together her bag, pens and papers, took her jacket from the back of her chair and left. Others in the group understood her distress but they were kept in their seats by their deep interest in the subject. It was becoming clear that unlawful behaviour can create a victim of anyone and the debate about the ways in which that might happen was fascinating.

Sometimes, Sarah still tried to ease hurt feelings by considering events from her sisters' point of view but she could not grasp their fundamental assumption. They were sure they were entitled to abuse her! If it was obviously due to casual parenting, surely as reasonable adults all that vitriol ought to be a thing of the past?

Sarah was looking for answers. Concealing the identity of her family, she discussed her worries with classmates during their coffee break. She had an attentive, interested audience. They continued the conversation as they returned to their seats and Nicole overheard some of the conversations Sarah's story had engendered. She abandoned her earlier dismissal to offer a new theory.

"Pack mentality can affect just two people!"

Sarah had hidden the parcel of documents out of sight but its contents were never far from her mind and the implications continued to affect her. She wanted to be free but felt unable to pull the package of documents from beneath her bed, even though she was often tempted to burn it to cinders in the fire!

The twins certainly worked together, albeit with an obvious leader in Mary. For the group, Sarah described the way the extortion demand was presented.

"The kisses and the drawing of flowers are there to tell you, *we aren't threatening really!*" she was advised. "It's to take the sting out of what they tried to do, trying to make you believe everything is fine. The message is, *we love you and here is a nice picture to prove it!* In reality, they just wanted your money." Nicole paused. "I'm sorry, Sarah …"

Sarah had guessed as much but it was saddening to hear the analysis. She noticed that Nicole sounded fractionally gracious, but she accepted the explanation. Her crestfallen expression was noticed by an elderly man who sat nearby. He had been scribbling notes but he looked up, peering over spectacles on the end of his nose. He made a short observation. "I don't see genuine love in this, Sarah!"

Another man agreed. "I'd be worried that you weren't warned in advance! Receiving the form must have been such a shock. It looks manipulative."

Sarah nodded. She could never escape the feeling that the twins tried to manipulate her; it had been true for as long as she could remember. The first man smiled at her. He had dark brown eyes and a kind expression. He sought for something else to say, obviously wanting to be supportive. "That might not mean they were actually being *evil* though!"

"Evil?" Sarah wasn't sure. The twins definitely thought they could force her hand but then, they always had! They were misguided by Lena when they were children but Sarah knew they both harboured only good memories of their mother. More recently, they were profoundly misled by Eileen, who was far more intelligent than they were. She had already wondered if it was in her heart to forgive them, because of it.

Yet there had been *so* much cruel talk from them and so many times she'd responded with a sickening lurch of the stomach. The most foolish of women do know when they are being spiteful! Sarah remembered Kathy's remarks about not turning the situation into a competition when all she had tried to do, was advise.

These had become repetitive thoughts. It would be easier to live with the possibility that Mary and Kathy were *not* evil! However, it seemed the classmates agreed, a calculated plan was behind the extortion demand. Kathy had been trying to make Sarah desist, so that Mary could carry on in their own way.

The group had questions. What did the two women look like? Were they identical? Did Sarah herself, look the same?

"No," she answered. With some vestige of loyalty, she did not describe them in detail. "They aren't identical twins although they are really similar to one another and they like to have the same clothes and hairstyles!" She pictured them in her mind's eye. "They're bigger than me!"

"Really, or does it just feel like that?" The pleasant, brown-eyed man glanced at Sarah over his spectacles. She remembered how she used to sit, hunched over her stories when Kathy and Mary bullied her and how, similarly, she felt their presence looming as soon as she saw the parcel of documents.

"It's both!" she said. "They insult me often, saying I have a nasty way of thinking!"

"Well, that isn't right!" said a dark-haired young woman, from across the room. "*You* aren't nasty!"

"It's a form of psychological projection!" Nicole declared. "They are being nasty …"

"Your voice is so gentle, Sarah," continued the younger woman. "I could listen to you talk for ages!" She paused before adding another generous observation. "You're pretty, too!"

"Thank you!" Sarah felt flattered but her train of thought went on, with this opportunity to express her feelings and some of her reflections about her sisters. On the subject of voices: "They speak in a high tone …" she said. "Sort of …"

"Childlike!" supplied the tutor. "It's to curry favour! Again, it's to seem non-threatening."

"And yet, it's quite dangerous, really," observed the brown-eyed man. He was seeing the discussion in a straightforward way, and that was the way in which the group was essentially led. Nicole had theoretical knowledge but she didn't seem inclined towards deep analysis.

Sarah replied. "I think I knew it! Yet, why do some people fall for it?"

"The important thing is, *you* didn't!" On that point, everyone agreed.

During another break towards the end of the afternoon, she was borne off to the cafeteria with a certain proprietorial air by some of her new friends. The man who had taken a close interest in Sarah introduced himself; his name was Jim. He had a deep suntan and Sarah thought he must live an outdoor life. Sure enough, when he bought coffee from the assistant at the counter, she overhead him chatting enthusiastically about his garden.

The students sat around small circular tables, turning their chairs towards Sarah, wanting to renew the discussion. A kindly Scotswoman named Maggie treated her to a cup of hot chocolate and Jim was keen for her to take a seat near the warmth of a radiator.

Sarah felt appreciative of their well-meaning gestures. As a single woman, she generally had to supply her own comforts! She sipped her drink, listening to the conversation around her, and it took an interesting turn.

"When you talked about your sisters' responses," Jim began.

"To my efforts to explain what we could do?"

"Yes. You said, they got angry. They told you everything was your fault, and said you were in the wrong. They seem to have said, you were the one who wasn't living in the real world?"

"It's odd!" Maggie put in. "Why couldn't they respect Sarah? Especially with her training?"

Jim followed his train of thought. "They just didn't want to! You know, there's a term for that behaviour and it fits with Nicole's projection theory. It's *gaslighting*!" He thought for a moment.

"Perhaps that's just the more colloquial way to describe it?"

The young woman who had spoken so supportively of Sarah, sat nearby. She had introduced herself at the start of the classes, saying her name was Penny. "Projection, is to try to deflect blame, isn't it? To make the second person think they are responsible for the first one's own feelings?"

Her companions agreed. "Pretty much!" Jim said. "So, if the first one is angry (for instance) they will make accusations that the second one is always angry … It makes that second person have doubts in a way that isn't fair."

"And gaslighting?" Sarah asked.

"There's a close similarity. The effort is to shake the victim's faith in his or her own perceptions. They want to make the victim think they are not living in the real world. They try to create a wobble about that person's sanity."

* * *

When they returned to the classroom, Maggie sat beside Sarah. She set out pads of paper, pens and textbooks on the long table in front of them. "You looked for a way to help your sisters, after what they did!" Musing, she went on. "I can't imagine how you managed that!"

Projection or gaslighting? The group raised the question. Nicole was used to discussions of this sort but she had an agenda of her own. She preferred being in control! Fortunately, she liked the topic and the challenge, so she began an explanation.

Psychological projection can be unconscious. It can be habitual. The tendency, formed in childhood, will be repeated inevitably when it seems to work in the child's favour; it is then continued as an adult. Perhaps it began as an attempt to blame a sibling for an argument or a fuss of some kind. The child was selfish, the sibling became upset, the child told a parent that the second one was the selfish one. It can be done in order to get oneself out of trouble or to avoid looking in the wrong.

In gaslighting, the perpetrators usually have a definite motive and there may be a plan of action at the root of their behaviour. To try to bolster their credibility, they will make accusations against the victim, with insults such as not being perceptive or realistic, having a poor memory, or experiencing abnormal responses to events and conversations.

"Yes!" Sarah had been asked what she thought she knew, even though she had information the twins could have used! Now, she reflected that their motive was obvious. They had set up a debt of three thousand pounds on the strength of Eileen's assurances. They were in awe of Eileen and could not contemplate the failure of their plan. When Sarah explained that the woman was dishonest, they chose to mistrust her instead! The twins wanted Sarah to be in the wrong; it was in their interests to attempt to create doubts of her own.

She remembered a particularly upsetting accusation from Mary. "One of my sisters said, my thoughts were distorted! They were not!"

"Her own ideas were the distorted ones!" Penny shook her head. "What a horrible word to use against you!"

"They needed Sarah to think they could be right!" Maggie remarked. "What is the very best thing to do?"

"Keep things simple," replied Nicole. "Spot attempts to manipulate you; recognise how cruel they are and absolutely refuse to engage in conversation or shared activities with those people. They won't change because they don't want to, so make that the end of it."

Sarah listened, thoughtfully. She had engaged with her sisters because she wanted to explain herself. She hoped to show them a better way forward with logical advice and (if only they had been open to it) her help. With hindsight, clearly, the effort was hopeless.

Maggie took a pen and began to write on a sheet of lined paper. After a minute or so, she set down her pen, opened a packet of sweets and pushed a couple towards Sarah along with the page. In curly lettering, she had carefully written out a few lines from a poem by Robert Burns.

"Oh, wad some Power the giftie gie us …
"To see oursel's as others see us!"

"Foolish notion," she said. "Seriously, I would have yelled at them! So, Sarah, don't be too hard on yourself."

* * *

A total of nine sessions comprised the college course, for which Sarah had booked her place at the start of the term. During the seventh afternoon, she began to notice something. The tutor was making subtle efforts to exclude her from group conversations.

Following the discussion that arose as a direct result of Sarah's description of her sisters' treatment, of course it was in the tutor's interests to move on and present the next part of her course. They left projection theory behind and began to discuss narcissist personality disorder. Sarah knew there was a strong possibility that Mary was affected by the grandiosity of a narcissist but she respectfully remained silent while Nicole outlined the theory. However, some of her companions remembered points they shared during the previous session and they raised questions for Nicole.

This should have led to worthwhile comparisons, since the questions were relevant and useful. It became clear to Sarah that, although Nicole addressed the theory of narcissism, she did not acknowledge the fact they'd touched on it during their examination of the ruthless selfishness of Mary. There hadn't been deep analysis but the discussion had caught the attention and the imagination of the whole group! Sarah had studied extensively as an adult learner; she had noticed the way students will appear to take on board the details of a theory only to discard it, sometimes even seeming to forget about it. At such times, she supposed that maintaining conversation on a theme could depend on a number of factors, including personal experience. The tutor's focus was a different matter; she had a certain duty to keep the attention of a class and Nicole would have retained Sarah's respect if she had been able to refer back to their relevant, prior reflections.

Distributing study sheets, Nicole was obliged to speak briefly to Sarah but she called her by another name! Sarah looked up in surprise. It was week seven! She saw Jim regarding her, with a humorous expression and he winked, when he caught her eye. Later, she walked with him from the building and they crossed the car park together. A breeze swept across the open space, ruffling his grey-and-brown hair and causing Sarah to shiver and draw her coat tightly around her. She paused for a moment, to fasten buttons. When she was ready to walk on, Jim amicably linked his arm in hers. She tried to match her pace to his long strides and he noticed, grinned and slowed down.

Jim referred to Nicole's behaviour. *"Sandra?"* He asked. "Is that what she called you? You know why she did that, don't you?"

"Oh, well …" Sarah demurred.

"Maggie was right!" He smiled down at her and they walked on, heading for the rows of parked cars. "You're very tolerant! Even so, you're a bit of a challenge for Nicole because you seem to know the theories already. She likes to be fully in charge of everyone!"

Sarah relented. There was no point in pretending she wasn't aware that Nicole had been dismissive, even rude. "Yes," she agreed. "Actually, I shan't argue with her but I wasn't keen on the way she made me feel. I think it's best if I call it a day!"

Jim stopped smiling and looked disappointed, so she explained something of her history. "I have studied in lots of places and my interests mean I sometimes cross over with the learning. I do end up listening to lectures I've heard before, in one form or another. I study online too. It never goes too well for me, if a tutor in a classroom setting takes against me!"

They had arrived beside her car. He released her arm and gave her a comforting hug, with a little pat on her back. He stood back then, and put his hands into the pockets of his jacket. She stooped to open the door before turning again, to face him. "I wasn't sure what gaslighting was …" She didn't want to seem disingenuous.

"I don't blame you for deciding that's enough!" Jim was very kind. "These community courses are interesting but often they're just something to do, to while away some time. I've seen people fall asleep during a class!"

Sarah smiled at that. She had witnessed the same thing. "Send me an email," she said. "We'll keep in touch, won't we?"

* * *

Narcissist Personality Disorder

(For the purpose of this explanation the narcissist is "he" "him".)
The individual who displays a narcissistic personality is suffering from an abnormal psychological disorder. The attitude of the narcissist is characterised by contempt for the wishes and the rights of others. Initially, this may be concealed in order to seem attractive and charismatic; he is often a deceptively sociable, outgoing person who seems to like his fellow human beings. When selfish, even ruthless behaviour emerges, it can look contradictory compared with what has gone before.

Some people never want to be the more forceful ones in a relationship, or in a group. They like to be led. When the narcissist's path crosses with theirs, he is able to develop and maintain a set of erroneous beliefs. Confident of being well worth knowing; sure of being leagues ahead of anyone else in intelligence and prowess, he may profess knowledge in many different fields.

Not simply vain or proud, the narcissist is under a powerful delusion, imagining superiority even when it cannot be shown to be the case. Convinced of possessing higher learning and better skills compared with his acquaintances, even when his superiority is *not* demonstrable the narcissist may be able to convince others of it and usually remains privately sure of it, regardless of how events unfold. He's likely to be lofty and disinterested if he makes a mistake and is called out on it.

He will welcome and thrive on compliments and praise, possibly affecting modesty. In truth, he expects to be admired. Narcissists can seem admirable, especially to pseudo intellectuals, using snippets of knowledge to impress and draw in those who are not discerning. Followers believe they have found a friendship to treasure but it is usually a mistake, for such heroes are flawed. Ruthlessly self-serving, as soon as there arises a difference of opinion or a conflict of interest the narcissist takes the best care only of himself.

The affected person (who may be termed *the sufferer,* since this is a psychological disorder which is not responsive to psychotherapy) may not value a relationship as deeply as he pretends and, in any dispute, will seem disdainful of another's upset, assuming a stance that is unjustifiably patronising. His reaction to challenge, regardless of how fairly it is expressed, may be grandiosity, followed by a display of unreasonable annoyance, even fury, in the face of another's determination.

If the narcissist's belief of superior knowledge is spotted as improbable and it becomes impossible to force someone to obey, he will become callously dismissive of the worth of that individual. Generally, he will not consider or address personal failings and this can be the case even when he is caught out in a lie. There may be apparent contrition but it's likely to be short-lived; it isn't genuine and before long someone who seems able to challenge the narcissist will be discarded. However, this change of heart often happens with lightning speed, with no evidence of regret and no vestige of fondness, even when a bond was thought to exist. The narcissist may express a certain disappointment in the one who confronts him but he will appear unemotional, creating a distance, failing to accept that he played a part in the collapse of the relationship. If the other person expresses dismay, he'll suggest they are weak, lacking forethought.

The narcissist cannot empathise with others, although he can act. He has no desire to reflect upon his own possible mistakes, even when harm was caused to another. Interest is lost; he will not assess his own impact and no attention will be paid to explanations, especially if they contradict a preferred point of view.

Mary

Mary thought she had legal expertise but she had none. She had scant knowledge of the role she was so keen to assume. She believed in an automatic right to act freely, even though her abilities and achievements did not support her belief that she knew best. It was an oddly selfish delusion for a person who was one of three sisters but perhaps it was unfortunate that her twin, Kathy always gave her unquestioning compliance. Blindly and foolishly, Kathy fed Mary's pomposity.

Mary may have avoided legal advice in the first instance in order to save money. It isn't uncommon for a layperson to imagine they can tackle something for which they haven't trained and where intelligent research is done carefully, sometimes there is a satisfactory outcome. However, there always needs to be that awareness of a need for information-gathering and an open mind, in case there are new details to learn. Forging ahead, even after Sarah raised serious questions, was unwise and showed Mary's difficulty in taking advice, especially from her sister.

Perhaps she suspected a solicitor would raise the same set of obstacles and issues? Why not be prepared to examine them? Was it possible that Mary knew her attempts to coerce her sister constituted unlawful behaviour? Did her extraordinary level of self-belief mean she could knowingly engage in the crime of extortion?

After she assumed the role of executor, Mary saw she couldn't convince Sarah of her entitlement, nor force the completion of her form. She became frustrated and angry, refused to listen to explanations and wouldn't accept guidance. She couldn't contemplate the possibility that she had made an error of judgement, so she insisted her plan was not flawed and believed it could have been put into action. Its collapse, Mary reckoned, was a direct result of her sister's ignorant refusal to comply. She made assumptions of superiority, refused to address the fraudulent nature of her activities, dismissed explanations and was therefore oblivious to any risk.

Mary's narcissism was absolute. She effectively discarded Sarah and smoothly moved on to a new target, an elderly relative who was taken in by her childish affectation of unhappiness. He settled the debt and this action eradicated any vestige of a chance of Mary losing her personal belief in her wisdom and supremacy. It had the same effect on the blindly copying Kathy!

Nicole
Some people develop a sense of power as a result of conducting lessons, imparting knowledge with which they are familiar and which is new to their students. School teachers who are regularly in charge of children are in a situation which, in itself, promotes a sense of superiority. It's especially true in primary schools where children are generally smaller than their teachers, but the same perception can also affect tutors in college settings. Students are older but they may be perceived as weak, even vulnerable and a certain type of tutor lets self-importance overtake reason.

Nicole displayed some typical traits of the narcissist. Having spotted Sarah's awareness of abnormal psychology, it seemed she felt uncomfortable. This could have been on an unconscious level but giving Sarah the wrong name after sharing seven classes with her looked deliberate. Modest tutors exist but there are those who dislike being challenged and they find it hard to acknowledge the prior learning which a mature student often brings to a class.

When a tutor is full of knowledge, their self-belief is likely to be well-founded. Nevertheless, a certain humility and openness to new ideas should always be present. Sharing knowledge with learners is a tutor's duty, while being receptive to their thoughts, beliefs and wisdom must be part of the whole picture in a learning environment. If the ability and the will to do that seem to be missing, then an element of narcissism could be present.

LATER

Months passed. In July, no birthday messages from the twins arrived for Sarah. Siding with one another, they bore a grudge and they kept it going, never wanting to address it. Neither Mary nor Kathy called, feeling uncomfortable, to suggest a get-together, a talk and an attempt to resolve their differences. She wasn't sent an invitation to her nephew's summer wedding and was saddened to think she was made to miss such a happy event.

Sarah felt ashamed of her wider family; the cousins, the nieces and nephews, the elderly aunts and uncles, who all seemed to go along with the deliberate snub. No-one contacted her to express surprise or kind interest after she was absent from an important part of their history.

Her friend's words returned to Sarah's mind. *"Sarah, people probably won't believe them, though. I think you should take no notice of them."*

How much harm had the twins caused? A great deal, possibly … but Sarah knew it was important to let go of troubling speculation. Careless talk must have gone on but she could hardly begin a campaign of letter-writing to dozens of relatives, not knowing exactly what they were all given to understand!

She wondered what would happen to Jeff's ashes and knew he had not wanted them to be scattered; however, interment would entail further expenditure and Sarah felt fearful in case new messages came her way. Sure enough, regardless of damage already done, in September Mary and Kathy both contacted Sarah to say *they needed money* for interment of the casket!

It was an impossible request on so many levels and Sarah never tried to address it. Even an offer to share the cost could run them all into argument again, since the person to decide on the amount would inevitably be Mary. Sarah would only need to make a mild request to discuss plans or examine receipts, to find herself plunged again into accusations of being difficult! The plain truth was, she couldn't trust her sisters or risk involvement in any money matter with them, so there was really no alternative to leaving arrangements to the sister who so wanted to take sole responsibility for everything (except payment). Legal advice could have helped them all, with a logical, informed review from someone who was impartial and could settle the dust over the funeral costs and explain a new way forward. It was a wasted thought for Sarah, who knew the twins would furiously reject it, just as they did before.

By this time, Mary probably believed she had won her battles with Sarah on almost all counts. She could not persuade Sarah to finance her but she was successful in keeping control, first of the funeral and then the casket. Her determined exclusion of proper advice had been maintained and she couldn't recognise her own foolhardy attitude.

Sarah knew she couldn't bear to hear more harsh words. She was glad the temptation to hurl spiteful comments of her own had been resisted, somehow. Relenting on the form issue was never an option; her strength of will was essential. Yet, if the episode was a battle there was no pleasure in the part she won. She wished there had been no such perception.

Uncomfortable reflections persisted for a time, despite Sarah's brave resolution to let them go. She kept returning to the effects on her wider family, especially Uncle Bill. It occurred to her that (since the twins were sure they had been unfairly treated), while they felt free to discuss Sarah, she couldn't know what further trouble they could cause. Worrying over it was distressing and pointless; she was only guessing now. She was relieved the sisters' interest in herself had come to an end, along with their communications.

* * *

Sarah struggled with the memory of Jeff's emphatic wish that his final resting place would be near his parents. Since he had been unhappy for much of his childhood, this revelation of love for Lena and Eddie seemed especially poignant. She thought about the disappearance of his possessions. Where had he saved the drafts of his story? They could have been stored in files saved to the new laptop, although he had mentioned "scribbles" and perhaps sheets of paper had been scattered in his home, unrecognisable as treasure to a casual observer, or the twins.

Letting go of the correct procedure was very difficult all over again, as she longed to sort everything out properly but it was painful to know that further efforts to bring order into matters would meet with fury from Mary and Kathy. An outright challenge of their control would surely be hellish. Minus conscience, they seemed certain they were above the law.

Sarah was keenly aware that possession of a signed extortion demand gave her power. The kisses and flowers which Mary had added to the page, counted for nothing. Certainly, they created no sentimental value! In fact, considering the intention they were supposed to mask, the reverse was true; it was a hateful letter. For anyone to imagine Sarah was foolish enough to buy into such nonsense was an absolute insult and, months on, her heart was hardened still further. Nothing could detract from the dangerous import of the letter but she suspected a legal action would result in more trouble than it was worth.

* * *

On a stormy evening in September, Sarah drove to the university campus and found a parking space behind a tall block of students' flats. A gust of wind blew raindrops in her face as she emerged from her car. She tucked her chin inside a woollen scarf, locked the car then turned and followed a path for a short distance before, choosing a short-cut, she crossed a strip of soaked grass and headed for the main building.

She was there to attend a seminar. In her hand, she clutched the stapled pages of a schedule. The first lecture was entitled *Mourning and Melancholia: A Freudian Theory*. It would be presented by a member of the department for psychoanalytic studies.

Sarah found the hall she needed and stood for a few moments in a reception area, divesting herself of the damp scarf. Her trouser hems were wet, too. She smiled at the secretary, who was checking the names of participants against a list. The woman recognised her and added a tick to the page.

Sarah went quickly up a flight of stairs and took her place with other students in a spacious lecture theatre. Glancing around the room, she saw people of varying ages and they chattered, then hushed and settled to listen to the talk. Sarah had been looking forward to the evening; despite some logical reservations, she knew such analytical presentations inspired useful comment and reflection afterwards.

A dark-haired young man dressed in a grey suit walked onto the stage. He placed a sheaf of documents on a small folding table, introduced himself as *Signor Barcia* and prepared to present his talk about grief and loss. The Italian professor had a strong accent but his command of English language was good. He spoke in an animated way and Sarah paid close attention to his words.

To begin with, Signor Barcia talked about the ways in which whole groups of society respond to outrageous war crimes. In their turn, those who express anger may vilify entire bodies of people whom they perceive to be collectively responsible for the crimes. He remained with the opening subject for a few minutes. Next, moving on to individual responses to grief, he explained that, when someone has feelings of sorrow, they may also demonstrate anger without an obvious cause.

Signor Barcia showed how outpourings of emotion can lead people to be creative. For instance, artists and sculptors often enter into a phase of their best work after a great loss. When there is inability to find an outlet, there may arise a destructive force. He highlighted the problem of guilty feelings after bereavement and especially their power to cause damage, both for the sufferer and those around them. Guilt, said the professor, is an inevitable part of the grieving process.

Sarah's imagination was captured! She considered the fact that none of the three sisters kept in touch with Jeff for many years and it was not until he became ill that he contacted them. He reminisced about fascinating, exciting experiences but had he missed his family? Was he lonely and would he have responded to sisterly concern and sought health checks, instead of postponing them until there was no hope of recovery? Yet, how does one keep in touch with a determined runaway?

Signor Barcia explained that unconscious processes cause a bereaved person to suffer emotionally and reproach himself.

"Or herself" thought Sarah! She had a question. She waited while two students raised their hands, were acknowledged and encouraged to voice their queries in turn. They received considered responses. At last, driven by her need to find a point of view she could live with, Sarah was next to raise a hand, although she could feel her heart racing. The professor gave her his polite attention; she took a deep breath and found her nerve.

"In a family situation, where there's distress as a result of a traumatic death, might the need to apportion blame be worse? Might it be so painful to bear the guilt, that it gets thrown at someone else? Projected onto a member of the family, a relative who seems to provide some kind of excuse to do that?"

There was a silence. Several students looked at Sarah then turned back to the speaker with interest. Emphatically, he agreed. "Yes!"

He glanced down, shuffled documents on the desk before him and selected a single sheet. Looking up again, he went on. "The projection is, of course, most deeply complicated by self-reproach. If the bereaved person feels sure he failed the loved one, he will certainly be angry, not just with himself but also with others. He is desperate to share the blame!"

Aware her companions were attentive, Sarah offered extra detail. She had been feeling overwhelmed by her family who were suffering grief over the loss of their brother. The twins felt sure Sarah was to blame for their frustration and annoyance with a process but in reality, it could not be altered. Again, she halted. She wondered if, protesting too much, she sounded like a person who *was* to blame! However, she had a fair listener now.

The good man answered enthusiastically, for he was writing a paper on this very subject! It was quickly clear he was better educated than Nicole, the tutor who saw just the tip of this emotional iceberg. Of course, grieving relatives are suffering emotional pain, but where there exists regret too, they are certainly likely to feel guilty and try to focus it, even hurting someone whom they see as challenging. Nicole had taken a common, dismissive approach, indicating that everyone in a scenario where argument arises is likely to be at fault, expressing their grief blindly. Signor Barcia understood the matter better. There was a victim.

"When this happens …" Signor Barcia looked at Sarah as if he knew the truth. "Ultimately, the victim, being blameless, will be *triumphal!*"

* * *

As soon as the twins targeted Sarah for their route to payment, a toxic battle began. The course of events couldn't have been different while their plan was impossible and it was always impossible. Sarah offered clarity and when she was rejected, she had no reason to give in, nor did she need to hide. She was entitled to attend the funeral but her heartache had been worsened immeasurably by her sisters' behaviour.

The professor smiled at Sarah with kindness in his eyes and it was a powerful, almost surreal moment. She would never forget his comment. He had been discussing war and war crimes before going on to examine the destructive forces of grief, anger and guilt. His topic had shifted from whole groups of people, even populations, to individuals and the various demonstrations of their pain. The expression of grief might be creative, or it might find no such outlet and a battle is the result.

So, Signor Barcia used the word "triumphal" in a literal sense, in that it can mean "victorious". Sarah felt a little thrill of pride. Yet, prior to that moment, she hadn't felt a sense of triumph over her sisters and upon reflection, in terms of its connotations of pride, the perception didn't linger. For sure, she was in the right. She had been forced into a type of battle but she fought with an educated aware-ness. Not blinkered or deluded like the twins (especially Mary) her responses had been founded on logic not passion.

The twins were not interested in Sarah, herself, during the argu-ment about their form. Her efforts to explain her decision were thought dull and pointless, especially since such reasoned argu-ments were beyond their comprehension. Their focus was on secur-ing money to pay a debt, set up with proper forethought or advice. When Uncle Bill was prepared to settle their debt, this was a gesture of kindness but the twins were unconcerned even on that point. His action satisfied them. Sarah's determination to reject their form was aggravating but with no emotional attachment to the process, they were not mindful of a personal battle. They simply fought for the money; however, they fought in the way they had developed.

In different ways, they had all tried to cushion their sorrow after their brother died. Wine played its part, since it does blur the worst misery of grief and this can be judicious to some extent. However, alcohol and levity may result in a veil being drawn over some important facts and they could need to be confronted in order to gain real peace of mind. An alcoholic haze is false happiness, after all! When depression hits again (and it will), so can the bad feelings. As Signor Barcia explained, there was guilt lying behind the fury within the family. Sarah understood. The sisters threw themselves at arrangements for the funeral because it was too late to help Jeff. Typically, it was Mary who loved to organise others; deprived of more time with her brother she needed to feel a sense of controlling *something*.

Sarah had agonised over a situation which (she knew) might have been dealt with in a straightforward way. To begin with, she could have thrown the parcel of documents on the fire. Afterwards, she could have completely ignored all her sisters' efforts to discuss the matter. It would have been a hard line to take and they would have been furious, but Sarah would have been justified. After all, she never really needed to assume the responsibility of trying to educate them! Unfortunately, problems would have arisen as a result of silence on her part and it was likely the aggressive telephone calls would have been maintained. Mary was very determined and Kathy was right behind her. So, her conscientious nature had led her on the path she took and she had tried to manage their onslaught in her own way. Trying her best to show honesty and reason; hoping for a better way forward, Sarah might have realised that such approaches would be lost on the twins.

In fact, to halt the sisters, there was a third option and it could have been used from the moment the significance of the document and the intentions behind it were clear; certainly, once the twins began to hurl insults. Sarah could have engaged a solicitor to peruse the forms and write to Mary, putting a formal end to her activities, once and for all.

What made everything so complicated? The causes were rooted in habitual attitudes and behaviour, which continued to follow certain patterns within the family. As a child, Sarah tried to avoid confrontations and even as an adult, although she felt she needed to address something that bothered her, she was endeavouring to be pleasant and harmless. When she began to try to explain her point of view and look for her right to be included in funeral planning, she hadn't understood the enormity of her sisters' resentment.

Sarah was not to blame for their animosity and she never deserved all the accusations. She had struggled with an element of fear, wondering if anything she did during the process begun by Kathy and Mary, was wrong. She had fought a terrible conflict within herself, especially considering that a stronger sense of self-preservation overall would have helped her. A flat refusal to acknowledge the form was a persistent thought and it refused to fade away, because it verged on regret. She would have saved herself the arguments with Mary and the spiteful remarks from Kathy. With a determined mindset against listening to the twins, Jeff's passing would have been a sad memory but events surrounding it might have been minimised. She couldn't turn back the clock and approach the situation differently, and when she honestly envisaged a scenario in which she ignored the arrival of the documents, she realised that she would very quickly have been plagued with telephone calls. Her sisters would have called her "irresponsible". They would have been able to accuse her of failing to at least try to explain herself. Beloved relatives like Bill would still have been affected and their understanding harmed, because Kathy and Mary would have insisted Sarah thought herself too good to share the burden of the funeral.

A precious memory lingered and it was the final talk with Jeff. Afterwards, she was able to support and care for him during his last hours. It was not her fault she was the only sister there. She was compassionate but the other two sisters had lost their opportunity; they were not present and had no chance to talk or join in with managing his passing. This made them terribly jealous.

Sarah's victory might have been perceived as incomplete, considering the twins could not acknowledge it. They would never understand her viewpoint or concern themselves with the true history of events. Nevertheless, she had resisted manipulation and a path to possible criminal investigation for fraud. She had been courageous and she was ultimately blameless. In all those ways, she had triumphed.

FINALLY

After Mary collected her brother's casket from the undertakers' offices, she kept it and insisted there were no funds available to pay for interment. She was touchy about the subject but since she had appointed herself executor and signed documents, it was a normal part of the process for her to assume responsibility for the ashes. After one enquiry, Sarah left her alone. It was impossible to try to change Mary's perception of herself and she was disinterested in the cruel effects of her behaviour.

The year wore to an end, a new one began and one afternoon in early spring, Sarah put on waterproof boots and a jacket to walk a short distance to a nearby river. Jeff loved to go to just such a peaceful place with his rods and other fishing paraphernalia when he was young. She carried with her a bundle of plants and a trowel. Soon she knelt, getting muddy and enjoying the scent of freshly turned earth, to plant blue forget-me-nots under a great oak. It was almost twelve full months since she learned of her brother's illness.

Sarah remembered a short prayer, which the children used to recite in primary school before they were released to go home. She murmured a few of the words, with the twittering of finches in nearby hawthorn hedges a background to her voice.

"Jesus, give the weary
Calm and sweet repose ..."

Then she walked away, following the stony path back to her cottage where her cat's triangular black face peeped through a latticed window. In the porch, she returned the trowel to a low shelf. She shed her muddy boots and coat before opening the door to the kitchen.

Sarah reached into a cupboard for a glass, which she placed on a counter before she went to the fridge to collect a bottle of white wine. She hunted inside a drawer for a corkscrew, found one and was then diverted by her cat's plaintive squeaks.

"Shush!" She set aside her preparations to pour wine, opened a cardboard box full of fish-flavoured treats and tipped some into his dish, then watched him eat for a moment. At last, she dug the corkscrew into the neck of the bottle, twisted it and tugged until she could remove the cork with a pop. She poured her drink, took a sip and mused. "It feels like the worst is over ... and it's chilly enough for a fire, this evening!"

Sarah ran up the narrow staircase, went into her bedroom and knelt on the carpet to retrieve the bound parcel that was still hidden beneath her bed. She carried it to the fireside, ripped off the packaging and reached up to the mantelpiece for a box of matches. Tearing and crumpling pages, she used the both the form and the letter to light a fire.

It *was* a relief of sorts; yet, strangely, the significance of the action no longer seemed so great. Flames from the burning paper caught kindling alight and began to leap through criss-crossed logs. Sarah added the remnants of the package. Soon, comfortably seated near the modest blaze, she raised her glass. "To my brother!"

LONDON

Sarah and Jim exchanged email messages and sometimes he called her during the weeks after she withdrew from Nicole's course. They lived a few miles apart but the nearest town was a halfway point. They met in a cafe for the first time outside of college, when they shared coffee and sandwiches. Jim then became a comforting presence in Sarah's life. She knew he would like to spend more time with her and she was considering ways in which their future might unfold. She had lived alone for a long time! Before making changes to her life, there was something she wanted to do and she planned to do it by herself.

On Jeff's birthday in the year following his death, Sarah travelled to London and went to the street where he stayed in his friend's flat, before he had to enter the hospice. It was a cool day in March. She wandered around market stalls for a while, liking the thought that this was where her brother once walked. A fruit stall was tempting and she bought a fresh mango and stowed it, wrapped in white tissue, inside her shoulder bag. Another canopied stand displayed accessories and trinkets. Sarah bought a delicate silver bracelet that lay at the front of the heaps of pretty things, because it was decorated with a tracery of linked hearts.

Tiring, she found a bench and sat there enjoying spring sunshine, drinking frothy coffee from a paper cup. She allowed herself to sink deep into daydreams with a treasured memory of leading her younger brother by the hand along the short pathway from the bus stop to their primary school. They collected and pocketed horse chestnuts, which were scattered on grassy banks in autumn. Often, they lingered at a field gate where shaggy ponies stood, eyeing the children and hoping for treats.

The sun was bright but a persistent breeze was cool. Growing chilly, Sarah stirred at last. She felt glad of her heavy Aran sweater and thick jeans. She bent and pulled a jacket from her bag, shrugged into it and zipped up the front to the top.

It was easy to picture Jeff as the intelligent, sensitive man he became, walking along the pathways to buy bread, cheese and olives in the market, chatting to acquaintances and perhaps heading off to meet friends in some wine bar in the evenings. There could be people in the locality who knew him.

* * *

Sarah brought her mind back to reality with an effort. Standing, she found a bin for her empty cup, then shouldered her bag and walked on. She skirted a pile of cardboard boxes, stepped up a kerb, exchanged a smile with an elderly lady ... but in her mind's eye there lingered a vision of Jeff's attractive, smiling face and the long fringe of pale hair that fell into his blue eyes. Dressed in her boyish clothes, with her chin tucked into her collar she looked similar to the brother who was once there. A breeze began to gust along the street; she raised a hand to brush her fair hair from her eyes.

At the front of the old building where Jeff once lived in his friend's flat, Sarah stood, forlorn despite her brave plans. She watched as a couple ran out of the door and hurried away, arm-in-arm. They were followed by an elderly gentleman, who smiled politely when she asked: "Excuse me! I wonder ... did you know a man named Jeff, when he lived here?"

No. He was new to the area, the man explained, before he wished her a good morning and left. She turned and walked away from the immediate pathways and the market stalls, until she came to a narrow frontage where a sign depicting wine bottles, French bread and cheeses tempted her inside.

The interior was a slip of space, with the serving area situated at the far end. Small square tables were neatly covered in red-and-white checked cloths. There was a fragrant aroma of coffee and the faint sound of classical music.

Sarah made her way to the glass-topped counter, where a tall young man with dishevelled dark hair waited while she deliberated over a selection of filled rolls and surveyed a blackboard bearing a chalked menu, before deciding to order a slice of hot quiche, salad and a glass of white wine. Then, turning back she chose a place to sit. There were no other customers and the bistro, which she had entered via several downward steps, was quite dark. Relaxing, Sarah stared abstractedly at a collection of paintings hanging on the whitewashed brick walls.

After serving Sarah's lunch, the owner of the bistro sat nearby, pencilling figures and frowning over his cashbook and calculator. Eventually, with a sigh, he pushed aside his work and sat back in his chair, rubbing his eyes with his fingers. A young woman, swathed in a pristine white apron over a dark top and trousers, walked briskly from the darkened regions behind the counter and set a steaming cup at his elbow.

"Thanks, my dear." He reached for it, absently linking his fingers in the handle while the coffee was too hot to drink.

"Bonjour!" The woman nodded at Sarah. She was petite, with short black hair. Standing nearby, she raised her arms to open and adjust a frilled white curtain over a narrow window.

Sarah had finished eating. She ventured to ask her question. "Excuse me … I would like to ask you something. Has *Jeff* ever come in here?"

The man glanced at her, raising his eyebrows in surprise. "Yes!

Do you mean the fair guy?" His expression changed to one of sadness. "He got ill though … he died."

"He did," she said. "I know, because he was my brother."

"Tiens!" The woman faced Sarah and rested a hand on a chair back for a moment, as if to steady herself. "Et comme vous êtes tellement … enfin! You look so like Jeff! We were very sad when he passed away."

The couple introduced themselves; their names were Tim and Cherie. Sarah answered their questions and was able to tell them that she comforted and supported her brother when he needed her. "It seemed little enough." She had not been able to describe to anyone that dreadful sense of helplessness in the face of her brother's weakness.

Tim had a point of view about that. "You were there," he said. "You talked to him and you must have really comforted him. That's wonderful, Sarah!"

He ran a hand over his tousled hair, then with a gesture he indicated a watercolour displayed on the wall near her table. It was a gift from Jeff, he told her proudly, as she got up to inspect it in the cool light that filtered into the room. The picture clearly bore a signature in the corner of the canvas and she exclaimed. "Oh! Jeff hardly ever signed his paintings!"

Tim stood, scraping his chair as he did so. "I asked him to sign that one," he said. "I tried to get him in the habit of it. He was good!" He stacked his notebooks on the counter with the calculator placed neatly on top and went to join Sarah in front of the painting. "After poor Jeff had passed away," he went on, "two fat women came and took everything out of the flat. They dumped some nice stuff on the path, for the charity shop to collect."

"We were worried," added his partner. "There was decent crockery and many new pans. We did not touch them, *naturellement!* I saw a bundle of papers being thrown into a rubbish bin, and I went to see what they were …" Abruptly, she turned and went into the back of the bar.

Tim regarded Sarah, whose inner child was still shamelessly grinning because of his blunt description of the women. "I hope you don't think she meant private documents! They weren't accounts or bills," he explained. "Look!"

Cherie returned with a cardboard folder, from which she extracted sheets of paper which she carefully smoothed out to show Sarah that they were covered in line drawings. They were Jeff's pictures and each page bore a scribbled signature.

"The big painting is valuable now," she told Sarah. "Customers make us offers!" She hesitated.

"I think you should have it," said Tim. There was a silence while they stared again at the depiction of two small, fair-haired children, holding hands, standing near the edge of a calm, blue-green sea.

"It's lovely," Sarah said at last. "I think it's a picture of me, with Jeff. It should stay here as it was given to you." Her gaze returned to the sketches. "These are ... well, much more than I hoped for."

Something became apparent. With a thrill of excitement, she saw that Jeff had added handwriting beneath and around many of the drawings. She turned them over, and sure enough there was more, scrawled in soft pencil but legible. They were diary notes.

Cherie began to tidy the pages; it was agreed they were Sarah's and this time she did not demur. She felt as happy and comforted as if her brother had written her a letter and gratefully, she whispered *"Thank you!"*

She sat, staring at nothing at all for a few moments and her companions fell respectfully silent while her mind was on the day when, in her father's attic, she hunted vainly for Lena's personal possessions. There was no doubt the sisters kept cookery books and interesting novels but their mother's journals had probably been thrown away. Tim gave her a friendly hug, then he went to the bar, opened a bottle of Chablis and brought it, with glasses, to the table.

The couple were lively people; talk became animated and Sarah relaxed. They shared happy memories for an hour before she decided to make her way home. At last, she gathered her coat and bag, tucked the folder full of sketches under her arm and said her goodbyes. Her brother's memory was respected and his work was treasured and safe.

POSTSCRIPT

Another year passed. Sarah brought her extra studies to a close once she felt satisfied of sufficient learning to be a fully effective counsellor. She enjoyed listening and providing therapy to clients. A morning room in her cottage was furnished with flower-patterned armchairs, graced with vases of daisies or chrysanthemums and whether it was lit by summer sunshine or warmed by a fire in a small grate, it made an attractive place for visitors. Sitting opposite a counselling client who really welcomed Sarah's gentle support was one of her favourite occupations.

An important person remained in her life. He was Jim, the kind man who took such an interest in her story of the sisters' cruel tricks, and he had courteously begun to invite Sarah to join him in visits to coffee shops, or lunch in a restaurant, then a more adventurous trip when they went away to Norfolk for a long weekend. Sarah loved him. She didn't care about their age difference and when he proposed marriage, she was delighted. Her tiny cottage could accommodate a modest person like Jim; he shared her love of animals, and she was content.

They both tended her garden, where Sarah had grown flowers and made rockeries. Now, they added a vegetable patch and a fishpond. Garden centres, where they wandered about, deliberating over accessories for the borders and the pond, became all the more fun to visit because they were together.

Sometimes, they enjoyed the company of a dear, elderly lady named Eva, who lived next-door. In chats over cups of tea, the two women had touched on the sisters' antics occasionally. Talking with both Jim and Eva helped Sarah to put events behind her so that, by the second anniversary of Jeff's passing, she rarely thought about Kathy or Mary.

* * *

There came an invitation to a family gathering, which Sarah decided to attend. It would be a lavish affair in celebration of a twenty-fifth wedding anniversary. Guessing the twins would be there, she wondered how Jim would feel about the prospect of meeting her family.

On visits home, Celeste had met Jim and they were now good friends but the sisters were a different matter. Sarah considered this. With his handsome face, suntanned skin and tall stature, Jim was attractive. Just into his sixties, he was well-spoken and intelligent. Mary and Kathy would probably be jealous! She kept that thought to herself, letting Jim make up his own mind about the invitation (which was addressed to Sarah *and one guest*) and, in fact, he wouldn't let her go alone.

At first, it wasn't much, that happened. Someone remarked on Sarah's "lovely suntan" and when she explained it was gained simply while she looked after her garden during the summer, Kathy argued, pointlessly as usual, against her. The British weather had been awful for months, she said. Raining, mostly.

Then another guest mentioned something she remembered about Jeff. Sarah agreed. Yes, Jeff was very artistic. Mary interrupted in strident tones, saying she was wrong! Jeff only thought himself of any use as an artist, she insisted. Couldn't Sarah remember? Eddie didn't bother with his drawings.

Mary's tone was derisive. It was painful for Sarah to hear such

nonsense but the moment passed because, this time, Jim was ready
to intervene. He knew the twins were unaware of the saved diaries,
sketches and paintings but he would not create an argument. He
took Sarah's elbow, smiled and nodded at the twins without saying
anything to them before guiding his wife away.

"I see what you mean!" Jim's presence and his kindness comforted Sarah.

Moreover, the beautiful painting still hung on the bistro wall in
London and there was a portfolio full of the treasured sketches in
the cottage. Sarah had prepared a draft document, planning to create a story which would reflect all that she knew of her brother's
travels. It would be illustrated with his wonderful drawings.

Author's Reflections

Left Out (How does this make you feel?)

The following reflection is unapologetically about the behaviour of some *women*. In my experience, men don't do this in quite the same way. If it does happen, it is unlikely to be for reasons of spite.

People who leave you out of their plans when you really might have expected to be included, don't care how you feel. Schoolgirls and adult women are often capable of creating such exclusion. It is an unkind action that is rarely undertaken without *any* awareness of the distress that may be caused; however, it can become habitual and the initial cause may be forgotten.

The behaviour has its roots in pack mentality. Friends group together and by leaving you out, for some reason they have a sense that they are protecting that group. Even when just two people snub a third, they are consciously *or* unconsciously trying to protect themselves. They could be aware that you would like to join in but that awareness is lost or obliterated; they move on because the fact is, they prefer to exclude you!

* * *

Physical Exclusion

Cruel exclusion of one individual is something that happens in schools, within families, and via social media You discover something nice was planned but you were not invited, causing you to feel a painful sense of shock. There is something uniquely unpleasant about being the one who is left out by others. If it happened by accident, you wonder why you didn't cross their minds. If it was done on purpose, the possible reasons can cause you to obsess and worry, especially when (in gaslighting) you are given to understand that your perceptions are all wrong! You can find yourself wondering if an event that (it seemed) definitely occurred, was never a reality in the first place!

Getting over such treatment takes a great sense of self-worth. At its worst, group exclusion of one person, who might normally expect to share their experiences, can make some people (especially those who are very young) feel suicidal.

Emotional Rejection

They do not want to hear that you feel offended or hurt. In projection, they will probably turn any complaint around to accuse you, the person who raised the issue, of being selfish and trying to spoil their happiness.

As a matter of fact, the likely result of being called out is: they will leave you out more often! They'll hate any sense of discomfort, any hint of a feeling *you* might be right and *they* were not fair, and they will get together and make themselves feel better. (On this, of course, you should not care. These are not true friends!)

Self Interest

A school friend once told me she did not want me to go to a discotheque with her because I was too pretty! I didn't know what to make of it, at the time. We were both aged just sixteen. She had thick fair hair and sparkling blue eyes, was brilliant at mathematics and confident in class. I admired her. I didn't feel superior in any way. Shocked, I was too naïve to understand but I knew her words were unfair.

Perhaps a direct attack like this is preferable to sly avoidance or accusations about one's character! However, those who feign friendship when it suits them, then leave you out for the same reason, aren't friends. They are looking only to please themselves.

Another thing to spot in that group is that, if they feel ill, they will make sure you know about it and expect your sympathy. If you fall ill, you may as well expect scant interest, even silence!

* * *

Mary wanted to lead at all times. Kathy had become used to copying her twin; she was too lazy to attempt to understand another point of view and too foolish to spot that, as soon as she began to have natural responses to Sarah, Mary stepped in to stop her. Both twins bolstered their ego by convincing themselves that Sarah was the misguided one.

When Sarah would have demurred, Kathy's spite was unconcealed. She told her sister that they were not in competition. Sarah was to understand the twins saw no fight and were simply behaving logically. Actually, the reverse was true. Mary fought for supremacy without a logical foundation and Kathy fought to let this happen.

Mary hurled a rude accusation that Sarah suspected a conspiracy. She meant to demean her sister with a suggestion that such suspicion was unfounded and small-minded. In reality, Sarah had guessed the truth. It wasn't a delusion invented by a troubled mind; a conspiracy was *exactly* what had happened and being caught out was the cause of Mary's fury!

* * *

How to cope?

This could be something to dismiss or, following natural disappointment, to come to terms with. A philosophical reaction is the best style for the scorned person who can, of course, make every effort to create such a good life of her own that bullying behaviour may be ignored.

However, if you find yourself regularly turning the other cheek and letting duplicitous so-called friends into your life at different times, there will always be an elephant in the room. They will refer to some shared excursion, party or event; you'll remember that you weren't able to join in and your sense of confusion will return.

If you complain, it's an opportunity for those who favour projection to try to fight with you and, if you are unlucky enough to be dealing with really spiteful people, their horrible response could come with lightning speed! Here (with the unspoken conversation to which they will not admit) is how it goes:

"We are so weak that you present a challenge to us, so we can't include you but if you complain, *we say you are weak for worrying about what we do.*"

"We were unkind when we left you out, you say? *We think you are unkind to get on to us! How hurtful you are!*"

A thoughtful argument is not *nasty*, even when it is not what the recipient wants to hear!

In counselling, especially in person-centred practice, the therapist aims to empathise and understand that every individual has their own perception of the world. A client should be able to offer their experiences and be heard without being judged.

In an argument between friends or relatives, both will be seeking an outcome that suits them. Nevertheless, each person in disagreement could be asked, fairly, to respect the point of view of the other. Perhaps most human beings in normal social contact would admit they find it hard to be patient when they feel strongly about something but reasonable people look for an outcome that is fair.

A narcissist might declare his opponent has a point, but in fact he'll believe he (the narcissist) is the one who is right.

If spiteful rejection is the only response you get to your feelings or beliefs; if it is damaging you and the people who cause you such unhappiness will not listen to your protests, then *you* don't need to feel bad as a result. In fact, it is a pity to mind too much because you can be sure they are nothing like as upset as you feel! You were the one who tried to express strong feelings. They haven't as much interest in the issue and they certainly haven't *your* best interests at heart.

A continued friendship or association with people who cast you aside so readily is likely to be baffling. They will be quite pleasant next time you all meet, because they are not the ones who suffered. In projection, they hurled accusations they did not mean or cannot be bothered to review; they just wanted to stop you making them feel guilty. It is important to recognise that these may not be true friends. If you move on and discard them, you will be happier.

When you make new friends after an experience with jealous people, you will be astonished by how much fun there is to be had. There will be no need to fight for a place in the group. A deeper analysis of the reasons behind one set's liking for you and another's dislike can be complicated, or it may seem to have no rhyme or reason! So, perhaps finding the courage to let it all go is the best strength of all.

Jesus, give the weary
Calm and sweet repose;

Sabine Baring-Gould 1834–1924

If you would like to send feedback to the author, please do!
lisaskeet@live.co.uk

Milton Keynes UK
Ingram Content Group UK Ltd.
UKHW012025120124
435957UK00010B/156/J